W9-BMY-776

The Elementals

Other Books by Saundra Mitchell

The Vespertine

The Springsweet

Shadowed Summer

The Elementals

SAUNDRA MITCHELL

HARCOURT
Houghton Mifflin Harcourt
Boston   New York

Harcourt is an imprint of Houghton Mifflin Harcourt Publishing Company.

www.hmhbooks.com

Text set in Cochin LT Std.

Library of Congress Cataloging-in-Publication Data
Mitchell, Saundra.
The elementals / Saundra Mitchell.
pages cm
Companion book to: *The Vespertine*, and, *The Springsweet*.
Summary: In 1917, Kate Witherspoon, who has lived a bohemian life with her artist parents, goes to Los Angeles where she meets crippled midwestern farm boy Julian Birch, another runaway, and together they realize they have the ability to triumph over death and time.
ISBN 978-0-547-85314-7 (hardback)
[1. Supernatural—Fiction. 2. Runaways—Fiction. 3. People with disabilities—Fiction. 4. Friendship—Fiction. 5. Motion picture industry—Fiction. 6. Death—Fiction. 7. Time—Fiction. 8. Hollywood (Los Angeles, Calif.)—History—20th century—Fiction.] I. Title.
PZ7.M6953Ele 2013
[Fic]—dc23
2013003904

Manufactured in the United States of America

DOC 10 9 8 7 6 5 4 3 2 1

4500405968

For my mom. Sorry for all the times I interrupted *Magnum P.I.*

Chicago, Illinois

1893

Prologue

Ordinary girls are untroubled by destiny.

Unfortunately, neither Amelia van den Broek nor Zora Stewart Birch was entirely ordinary. They leaned against the dining counter, watching the whole of the world grow smaller as they rose into the air on the great Ferris wheel.

Incandescent bulbs twinkled all around them, captured stars that illuminated the car and its sparse elegance. Seats with velvet cushions and wire backs filled the gallery, lazily spinning with no one to sit in them.

Tearing off a bit of fried dough, Amelia pointed toward a white-columned building in the distance and said, "That one right there. You should go look at the murals; I helped paint them."

"How many talents do you have, Amelia?" Zora asked.

With a snort, Amelia popped the dough into her mouth and said, "Too many. I see the future, I rise from the dead, I'm forever *not* strangling Nathaniel."

"So your temper's improved."

Amelia laughed. "Hardly. I quarrel instead of strangle, and he does the same."

Her eyes trailed to the corner of the car. Her Nathaniel leaned against the wall, talking to Emerson, entirely ignoring the view outside the window. He could travel on the wind; he had a sick and regular habit of jumping from heights for the thrill of it. Seeing Chicago and its World's Fair from a locked car didn't interest him in the least.

After a moment, Zora pressed a finger against Amelia's nose, then laughed at her dazed expression when she tore her gaze away.

"You're such a liar," Zora said, marveling. "You're still mad for him."

"I am, I admit."

"Good," Zora said. "We needed *one* good thing to come from all that."

In reply, Amelia kicked Zora's foot and let that speak for itself. *I have you,* it said. *And you have me as well.*

"Mean," Zora said, then clutched the counter. She wasn't sure she liked the view from this distance, and when the car swung ever so slightly, she startled. It turned out that she was a ground-beneath-the-feet sort of girl. Skyscrapers didn't interest her, and she had learned to dislike the crush of cities. Even though darkness mostly disguised Chicago that night, it made little difference.

Toward the east, thin fingers of lightning stroked the sky. It was a storm so removed, it seemed more decoration than threat.

Amelia frowned at it. Then she asked, "Does it worry you?"

"Not especially." Smoothing a hand down Amelia's sleeve, Zora smiled. "I'm not in the middle of it; I didn't command it. So I think it has better things to strike."

They'd had days to unburden themselves, to make confessions and share new secrets. They'd spent hours acting like children, spending pennies on Magic Lantern shows and sneaking into the opera, riding the train together, perched on top.

Pretending this visit would last forever, Zora would still sometimes grow sober and exchange a look with Amelia. A room was different when four of them shared it. Not *bad*, but not right, as if everything trembled on the edge of explosion.

Amelia smiled crookedly. She felt the balance shifting and tried to cling to her best friend just a little longer. "I've been thinking. We could be the most remarkable wonder of the world if we wanted. A full circus, contained in four bodies."

"We could call ourselves the Glorious Elements," Zora agreed. It would never happen, but they could spin fables about it.

"Barnum and Bailey would beg us to travel with them."

Spreading her hands out, Zora imagined the headlines. "A spectacle for the ages, see the gifts of the ancients performed before your very eyes."

"We'd be world famous!"

"And rich!"

Throwing her arms around Amelia, Zora pressed their brows together. In a sudden, quiet confession, she said, "It frightens me sometimes, the things we can do."

"The only reason it doesn't frighten me," Amelia confided, "is that I refuse to look anymore."

Zora loosened her grip a bit. "I'll look, but I won't call it."

"Is Emerson careful?"

"Oh yes." Zora caught a glimpse of Emerson sprawled in one of the plush seats. He rubbed his own knees idly, his face turned up to listen as Nathaniel held forth. "It would be easy to ruin good land if he weren't thoughtful. Between us, I'm the reckless one."

Dark eyes lighting up, Amelia laughed. "Which means you're both ridiculously steady. Practically dull, even."

"I resent that," Zora said. "I stole a horse once!"

"Once!"

Falling quiet, they held tight as the wheel finally crested its greatest height. The fair below was nothing but bright sparks of electric light. Chicago was a silhouette against the distant storm. In that quiet, crystallized moment, trembling in the sky, caged in glass, they both feared this was the end for them.

Zora was married; Amelia planned to never be. One settled, the other wild, there was no reason for them to meet again. They would have to tend their friendship carefully if they wanted to keep it.

Interrupting them, Nathaniel tucked his yellow handkerchief back into his pocket and held out a hand. "We should go before the rain catches us."

Amelia squeezed Zora once more, then turned to whisper in her ear. "Promise me this won't be the end."

Shaking her head, Zora pulled back to meet her gaze. "I swear it."

Coming to join them, Emerson slipped an arm around Zora's shoulders. "Good to meet you," he said, and he meant it in an abstract sort of way.

The car was empty save for their little group, so Nathaniel didn't bother with discretion. He unlocked the door, opening the car to the night sky. They still dangled above the fair, all its white lights miniature and blinking below them. Pulling Amelia close, Nathaniel nodded his goodbyes. Then he twisted the wind and they jumped. They disappeared, swallowed by the signature of Nathaniel's magic: the black void and gold stars.

From without, Zora and Emerson stared at a space that was simply, suddenly unoccupied. The explosive edge to their meeting faded, and Emerson relaxed. Brushing a kiss against Zora's hair, he held her tight when she curled toward him. "Was it a good visit?"

"Yes," Zora replied. She closed her eyes and pressed her face against his shirt, breathing him in until the ache inside her faded. The hum of gears filled her ears, her skin prickling with the heat she drew from Emerson's body.

Somewhere in Washington Park, Amelia and Nathaniel stood beneath the glow of a phosphorescent lamp. Trees whispered around them, turning their leaves to stretch for the coming rain. With water in the air, and the rivers that wound through town, they'd have to walk for a while.

Since they didn't yet know where they were going, a walk before a storm suited Amelia's mood exactly. She wasn't an ordinary girl; neither was Zora.

Destiny waited.

Connersville, Indiana

1906

One

The first time Julian Birch died, he was six years old.

It was autumn, precisely, just before it was time to mow the harvested cornstalks down. They stood sentinel in the fields, papery and gold. Stretching toward the horizon, they could be endless — and frightening. With each breath of wind, they hissed. They whispered at night. They towered and shook sharp fingers, and quivered. They were terrible.

Sometimes, Julian sat in his eldest brother's window upstairs. From there, the cornfields didn't look like a menacing wall. The stalks stood in their rows, trapped in neat lines, separated by gullies. It was only corn, good to eat for boys and pigs alike, nothing dangerous at all.

When Charlie found him at the window late in September, whispering to the fields, he went to carry him back to bed. Julian shivered all the way to his room. The walls bent toward them; dark faces appeared in the flowered wallpaper, baring their awful teeth. Pressing his face to Charlie's shoulder, Julian didn't want to let go.

"All right, bedtime," Charlie said.

Julian clung to him, croaking, "My head is broken."

With that, Charlie carried him downstairs, interrupting his parents' reading. Each night, no matter how long the day, they always read together. Mama perched on Papa's lap; she whispered poetry against his cheek, and he murmured the almanac in reply.

This vaguely embarrassed the older boys, but they suffered in silence. They weren't invited to this ritual, and if they didn't want to see it, there was always plenty of work to do around the farm, even at night.

"Sorry," Charlie said, shifting Julian in his arms. "Found him upstairs talking to the corn. I think he has a fever."

Mama slipped to her feet, taking the baby and turning back in surprise. "Emerson, he's burning up." She still thought of him as the baby; her baby, golden-haired and brown-eyed, her favorite little sunflower.

"I'll get the aspirin," Papa replied, then looked to Charlie. "Go make up the sitting room for him."

Before dawn, Papa rode into town to fetch the doctor.

The doctor couldn't say for certain what the matter was, but with a fever so high and a child so listless, it could only be contagious. No one slept that night; Henry and Sam stuffed a straw-ticking mattress. Mama and Papa took turns bathing Julian with cold water from the well.

By dawn, Julian had a new bed in the pole barn. Mama arranged him on the mattress with the best pillow in the house. The ache in his head felt like a driven spike. It vibrated down his spine and stole all the strength from his legs. Mama came out with meals, but no one else was allowed inside.

Sam and Henry liked to run outside and knock at the walls. Sometimes they'd yell in if they found a toad or a snake or had had a good dessert at dinner. Charlie came, but Julian never knew it. He huddled by the door and peered at him through the crack.

The barn was sweet and quiet, filled not with animals but with hay. Light filtered between the boards, marionettes of dust dancing in the beams.

But for all that visiting, it was lonely, and he couldn't sleep all the time. Mama would come, breakfast, lunch, and dinner. She alone came inside. Knowing she'd soon be along to wake him made it easier for him to sleep.

At night, the corn whispered. It surrounded him,

stretching for him, dried and dead and hissing his name as the cool autumn moon passed by.

The only good thing about his prison in the barn was that he didn't have to walk all the way to the outhouse. He had his own pot. During the day, Mama carried it to him and took it away to be emptied. Julian didn't want to use it alone, not at night, not with the cornstalks pressing in from all sides. Mama would check on him eventually, but on the fourth night, he couldn't wait.

Rolling from bed, he collapsed. The bright green sting of hay dust hazed around him. His skin prickled; he wheezed breathing it in. Cool earth spread out beneath him, and if it hadn't been for the itching, it would have been nice. No more aching, no more burning — just pounded dirt, chilly at night and steady.

Still, it felt wrong to lie there. Pushing up slowly, Julian found that his arms held him, but his legs simply would not. They were soft as dough, and nearly as biddable. Collapsing again, Julian peered at the door. It was open the slightest bit — if he could drag himself there, perhaps Mama would hear him call?

So inch by inch, he dug his fingers into the dirt and scraped across it on his belly. A chill broke out on his skin, and sickness drove a new spike in the back of his head.

Though it felt like he had dragged himself for hours, it was only minutes, and barely half a foot. Wasted, his cheek pressed against the ground, he gazed through the open door.

Everything looked wrong. Too blue, turned the wrong way. Then he saw a scarecrow carrying his mama through the yard. The field's terrible rasp wavered, filling the night and washing over him. Julian opened his mouth and shaped the words *Mama, help! Papa, please!* But no sound would come out.

Pain thundered through his head and, exhausted, Julian stilled. He lay his cheek against the floor and exhaled. A dead beetle spun, its husk rattling in the quiet. Blinking slowly, Julian blew on it again and watched as its spindly legs flickered. Righting itself, the beetle skittered into the shadows, leaving Julian entirely alone.

His chest quieted, no heartbeat and no breath. The corn quit whispering; his skin stopped aching. Everything went black.

But then, like a lantern starts with a spark and slowly glows, an ocean crept in. Sound came first, the rush of water chasing earth. Salt spread over Julian's tongue, thin and liquid as waves stretched to fill the dark.

He'd never seen the sea, but he recognized a beach all the

same. Rocky outcroppings framed the water with sharp edges. Mist cooled his skin, and he made out a silhouette, barely discernible in the night.

Dark hair spilled from a cap, one silver lock fingered by the wind. A thread of fire traced the horizon, revealing a curve of hips, a hint of a smile. The sweet scent of honeysuckle swept around her.

Holding out her hands, she waited. She was tall and pretty and very grown-up, Julian thought, so he didn't understand why she was waiting for him. Her lips moved, but his father's voice spilled out.

"Wake up, Julian, wake up."

And then it burned. Everything — the girl, the ocean — peeled away in flecks of char and ash, and when Julian sucked in his next breath, he sputtered. Lungs searing, and pain thundering back through his limbs, he cried when Papa shook him.

Tucked back in his bed, Julian pressed his face against his father's rough shirt and shivered the rest of the night through. He was safe from the corn, from the dark, from the ocean — and he dozed as a black beetle rustled through the hay beneath his head.

That was the first time Julian Birch died. But it would not be the last.

Al'Uqsur, Egypt

1906

Two

At five years old, Kate Witherspoon had no concept of time.

Gliding down the Nile in a flat-bottomed boat had taken forever — at *least* forever. Surrounded by silt-dark water, she watched for snakes (she saw a few) and alligators (she saw none, though claimed at least four) and waited.

Her parents bickered fondly over the heat, whether they should drink wine or water, about mummy dust and herons' wings. It got especially silly when Daddy pointed out it was rather late in the year for the river to still be so high.

"It doesn't seem especially flooded to me," Mimi replied.

Daddy slowly turned to look at her. "Have you been down the Nile very often?"

"As often as you."

With a lovely, low murmur, Daddy said, "You'll argue about anything."

"I will not!"

Pointing at the sky, Daddy demanded, "What color is it, Amelia?"

Mimi lifted her chin. "Orange stripes, obviously!"

That made them both laugh, and Kate sighed. The boat ride was supposed to be exciting. *Egypt* was supposed to be exciting. This was just sitting and mosquitoes and nobody paying attention to her for forty million years. At *least.*

The boat slowed. Then it bumped and thumped, still tugged by the current until the captain tossed a thick rope to a man on shore. Quick as could be, they tied the boat off, and Mimi tugged Kate's ear as she stood. "We're here; isn't it wonderful?"

Surrounded by green fields and blue sky, Kate didn't see anything wonderful. It was more nowhere.

Porters carried their luggage as they stepped from the boat. Palms pointed the way, a path worn through the cotton and papyrus fields. Climbing onto a waiting camel, Daddy took Kate in his arms. She was his tiny queen, a miniature of his beloved in pinafores and ruffles, so he sat her in front to give her the best view.

"What do you think?" he asked.

The novelty of riding camelback had worn off when they'd gone to see the pyramids and the sphinx. To Kate, this place looked no different from the rest of Egypt. It was lushly green near the river, and tawny sand everywhere else. Obviously, Daddy saw something special here, so Kate did her best.

"It's quiet," she said. "Will I have to be quiet?"

"Absolutely not."

"Also, I think there are snakes."

"Do you?" Daddy smiled. "I wouldn't play with them, if I were you."

With a sigh, Kate leaned against him. "I should like to play with a monkey."

Mimi caught up, slipping a lacquered chopstick into her hair to keep it off her neck. She didn't bother to hold on to the saddle at all. She rolled with the camel's long gait as if she'd been riding them her whole life. "We already discussed this. No monkeys unless you catch one with a ribbon."

"What if it follows me?"

"Following, no." Mimi glanced back. "Capturing, yes. Those are the rules."

Daddy waited until Mimi was out of earshot, then said, "Rub a bit of banana on the ribbon. That'll help."

Their camel lumbered on, hot and pungent beneath them. The march to camp was a parade of old, broken things. Daddy seemed fascinated, pointing at rubble and ruins in delight. Later, Kate would remember none of it, but she did like having all of her father's attention for the too-short ride.

Suddenly, he shifted behind her and pointed past her shoulder. "Look, pet."

Silk pennants snapped against golden mountains and lapis sky. Someone had built a pavilion between two massive statues; a polished wood floor rested between the colossi. Hooks ground into ancient stone held an awning high, and lanterns hung beneath it, waiting to chase away darkness once it crept in.

It was luxury in the midst of a desert, rich furnishings against the canvas of a long-dead empire. Exactly the kind of thing Daddy and Mimi enjoyed: worldly and other-worldly, entirely inspirational.

Daddy handed Kate down, then dismounted with a hop. "Go play, pet."

"Stay close," Mimi said. She was already busy unpacking: Kate's worn pillow, Daddy's cologne bottle, her own favorite shawl. Because they didn't have a house, she'd once explained, everywhere was home as long as they had their special things.

The air was dry and bright, a kind of startling hot that

burned shimmering waves into the distance. Hopping off the pavilion, Kate wandered to the base of the nearest statue.

If she tipped her head all the way back, she could make out the shape of a sandstone king at rest. He soared against the sky, sixty feet up and barely recognizable. His head and knees and elbows were left, but his face was lost to time. Daddy said one of the statues used to sing, but this one simply sat, staring blindly into the east.

Fitting her fingers into cracks, Kate scaled the pedestal. Grit stung her palms, and little black flies circled her head. It was much higher than she expected. Flopping on her belly, she inhaled dust until she caught her breath. From this height, she saw the path that led back to the river, all the colors of the fields, and more ruins. Everywhere, ruins!

Standing again, Kate walked past the king's toes. Then she measured herself against the lady statue that stood beside his thigh. She was much taller than Kate, and captivating because her breasts were bare.

Of course, Kate had seen real flesh bodies; sometimes models came to pose when they were in Paris. Mimi and Daddy both painted, canvases full of watery nude Aphrodites, long-thighed Ceridwens, Eves entwined with snakes.

But this was a bit different — a lot different! The statue was immense, her body half-polished, and most importantly, no one was looking. After weeks of being warned not to touch anything, Kate couldn't help herself. Straining, she squeezed little grunts from her throat, but she was too short.

Up on her toes didn't work. Stepping onto the sculpture's broken feet brought her closer. Mimi's laughter floated in the wind, and Kate froze. She turned, listening, waiting to hear it again. Palms whispered; the flies hummed, but no one called out to her. No one would stop her.

Steadying herself, Kate jumped. Sandstone, warm as flesh, slipped beneath her hand. She'd done it! Even as the wind tugged her curls and pulled at her hems, she celebrated. Feeling giant, she jumped again.

This time, stone crumbled beneath her. A slash of wet heat crossed her brow, and then she was on her back. Faerie lights danced in her eyes, motes that turned from silver to pink to red. When she opened her mouth, no breath came out and none would come in, but she wasn't scared.

Everything was odd. Above her, stone birds hopped on carved lines; etched flowers waved in the wind. Two men brandished tennis racquets and looked very proud. There were hands and cups, and even whole arms, suddenly washed in crimson. Mimi said they were hieroglyphics, a secret Egyptian language. But those fingers wriggled and reached for her. They were terrifying.

Kate was sure they'd grab her, snatch her right up, drag her into tombs full of dog-headed men and bird-bodied women. Because she'd dared to touch a stone queen's bosom, they'd keep her — forever and ever buried in the sand.

"No," Kate croaked. "Stop!"

And it did.

Everything did. No more wind; no more flies buzzing. The palms held their perfect fingers to the sky, none curling or quirking or swaying. All the voices stopped, camels fell silent, birds hushed. Shadows stopped crawling the throne; they became painted-on and immovable. Kate looked to the pavilion, where her parents should have been. They were gone. She was too stunned to cry.

Sinking down, Kate closed her eyes. Her head throbbed, and it wasn't just a feeling. It was a shade of dark that pulsed in her mind. It was almost like the dark when Daddy carried her on the wind. But there were no glimmering waves in it. It tasted of salt and sunset; it felt like velvet on her skin — and then there was a boy.

In one pulse, Kate saw him, pale hair and dark eyes. He reached for her, and in the next pulse, he was gone. Her eyes snapped open, and shadows jumped into place. The world flickered once, then began again. Sound and light crashed into her; rocks cut into her back.

Kate took a searing breath, and the first sound she made was a sob. More came, wrenching through her until she felt sick. Blood stung her eye; it smeared her hand when she reached up to touch it. As voices rang out, Kate struggled to sit.

With the faintest snap in the air, her daddy appeared and scooped her off the ground. He held her so tight, she couldn't breathe again. But that felt like safety; it smelled like his cologne. He swore against her hair that it was all right, she would be all right.

Mimi ran toward them, ashen and shocked. "Oh, God, Nate, she was only gone a minute!"

Which wasn't entirely true. She'd been gone for eight minutes, then lived another thirty seconds alone while time stood still in the pavilion. Kate had no concept of time, but the silvering of a single strand of hair proved that her body did.

Every second counted.

Everywhere

1917

Three

Julian groaned when his mother nudged him with a peck basket of green beans.

They came fresh from the garden, newly plucked from the vines. Each one would have to be broken in thirds and its string stripped. Next to washing dishes, snapping beans was Julian's least favorite chore.

Before he could complain, Zora said, "It's for your party. You can help."

"It's my birthday," he countered. "Can't Sam do it?"

"He could," Zora said. A smile touched the corner of her lips. "But I thought you'd want to be on the porch when Elise came by."

Grabbing his crutches, Julian hauled himself up. "Will you carry those for me, please?"

Zora only laughed, following him as he hurried to the back door. Elise Kidwell lived on the next farm over. Her family traded milk and meat for the Birches' fruits and vegetables. Today, it would be quarts of cream for the ice cream crank.

On account of the war, most families were going without meat three days a week, and eating gritty victory bread on all seven. Since the Birches grew no wheat, they made do with cereal bread, but they bartered for meat, and butter, and luxuries like cream.

Thumping across the porch, Julian dropped his crutches and slid them out of the way. Then he leaned against the rail, tucking his withered leg behind the strong one. Sunlight filtered through his blond hair, and when he turned to look toward the Kidwells' farm, it illuminated the long curve of his lashes.

He was built beautifully, with Zora's eyes and Emerson's strong jaw. Golden from working in the sun, he had a dusting of freckles on his nose, and a whole constellation of them on his shoulders.

"Thank you," he said, taking the colander out of the basket. "I'm all set."

Instead of taking the hint, Zora folded her hands and looked up at him innocently. "Now, you know you have to snap the long ones in fourths."

Julian stared at her. "Yes, ma'am, I know."

"And to save the strings and stems for the compost."

"Mom!"

With a wicked smile, Zora licked her thumb and reached up to smudge imaginary dirt from his face. When he recoiled, she laughed and went back inside. Her voice floated out behind her, before the screened door slammed closed on its own. "That's my baby sunflower."

Cheeks hot, Julian snapped beans with a vengeance and called after her. "I'm seventeen!"

"Not 'til tomorrow, cootie," Sam said from below. He yanked the hem of Julian's trousers, then darted out of reach. Two years older, he was the only other brother who still lived in the big Indiana farmhouse. The other two had a cottage out by the river and acted like they were grown men on their own.

Throwing his arms out, Sam cooed from a safe distance. "Baby sunflower. Bitty baby sunflower, teensy tiny sunflower."

Pointing at him, Julian said, "Don't make me knock you on your back seam."

"Is Elise coming over?" Sam took a few steps back. "Think she'll wear her war crinolines?"

Julian tossed aside a stem and reached for a new handful of beans. "No."

"I could stand to get a gander at her ankles again."

Though he kept his expression still, Julian simmered inside. There were plenty of girls in town for Sam; girls he'd gone to high school with, girls from church. Every year on the Fourth of July, he hopped from picnic blanket to picnic blanket. He came home stuffed with homemade rhubarb pie and, last year, with lipstick on his cheek. Julian cut him a black look; Sam didn't need to go gawking at Elise, too.

"Maybe she'll" — Sam wiggled his fingers suggestively — "do the hoochee coochee for you. Maybe she'll do it for *me*."

The fact was, Sam couldn't have cared less about Elise Kidwell. But Julian didn't know that for sure, which was why he grabbed his crutches and came off the porch like a bullet. There wasn't much room to run behind the house. Too far to the east, and they'd trample their mother's house garden. Too far to the west, and they'd end up in the chicken coops.

So Sam twisted like a dervish, just out of reach because Julian couldn't angle as quickly. Fresh with sweat and swinging himself around, Julian suddenly grinned. He didn't have to find more speed. Stopping dead in place, he stroked his fingers against the smooth curve of his crutch.

"Giving up already?" Sam taunted.

Julian grinned. "Too tired to keep up?"

Sam's high-pitched laughter rang out. He stopped, then

lunged toward Julian. Each time, he threw up his hands, trying to get his baby brother to flinch. His hazel eyes danced when he got closer, and then he made his fatal mistake. He leaned too far forward.

Wielding a crutch like a crook, Julian knocked Sam's feet from under him. Then, before he could get up, Julian hopped over and pressed the crutch's cotton-wrapped foot against Sam's breastbone. Not hard, not to hurt him. Enough to make the point that this skirmish was over, though.

"Uncle?"

"We don't have one," Sam said, refusing to surrender.

Pressing a little harder, Julian leaned over. "Say it."

"Uncle," Sam whispered, then grabbed the crutch with both hands and pulled. He paid for his cleverness when Julian fell on top of him, with an unintentional elbow to the ribs. They both lay there and groaned. Beans weren't being snapped, and no one was watching the side gate to see Elise let herself in.

The screen door snapped shut. Julian sat up, shoving Sam for being Sam. "Thanks a lot."

"Hey, you're welcome." Sam sprawled in the grass, tucking his hands behind his head. Careless and soaking up the sun, he waited for Julian to stand. Snaking a foot over, he poked the back of his knee with his toe.

Julian bobbled, but revenge would have to wait. Elise

appeared in the frame of the screen door, and she wasn't wearing war crinolines. Instead, it was her usual dungarees and blouse — working clothes. The girls in town could go around in glad rags every day. They wouldn't be called on to deliver a calf or rewire a stretch of fence.

Raising a hand, Julian waited 'til she stepped onto the porch. "Afternoon, Elise."

"Afternoon, Elise," Sam echoed.

Elise bounded down the steps, brushing stray tendrils off her forehead. "Happy early birthday, Julian."

Warming from the inside out, Julian smiled. "Thanks."

"Know what you're going to wish for?"

"I have a couple things in mind," Julian said. His smile stiffened slightly when Sam nudged him again. "You're coming to the barbecue, aren't you?"

"Wouldn't miss it."

"Me either," Sam said.

Since his crutches lay on the ground, Julian couldn't kick Sam for interfering. Instead, he fixed his gaze on Elise and pretended his obnoxious brother didn't exist. It wasn't hard, looking at her. The freckles in her hazel eyes entranced him. She cast spells with the curve of her lips.

"I'm glad. I'm looking forward to it."

"I hope you like your present," Elise said.

"You didn't have to get me anything."

A breeze stirred, tugging their hair and trailing the sweet scent of wild roses between them. Casting her eyes down, Elise was quiet a moment. When she looked up again, her expression was softer. So were her words. "I wanted to."

Sam pushed up on his elbows. "*My* birthday's next month."

The moment broken, Elise rolled her eyes and said, "How nice for you." She tugged Julian's collar, then backed off. "See you tomorrow."

Julian wanted to stay her. His bones and blood begged him to. He knew poetry, all sorts, romantic and classic. And songs; he could take his father's fiddle and sit beneath her window, make the night weep with a ballad for her. Instead, he waved, watching until she disappeared past the corn.

Sam rolled to his feet. Reaching over to chuck Julian's chin, he said, "Better shut your trap, baby sunflower. You're catching flies."

Still dazed, Julian brushed his hand away. "'Bout time for you to shut up, Sam."

"You kill me, kid. It's just Elise."

Julian didn't mean for the words to slip out; maybe if he'd been talking to Charlie. Charlie understood him better than anyone and never felt like he had to rattle his cage. But it was Sam standing there, so he's the one Julian told, "I'm going to marry her."

Picking up the crutches, Sam thrust them into Julian's hands and clapped him on the back. "You should try kissing her first."

It wasn't bad advice.

~~~~~~

The trouble with stealing her father's clothes, Kate decided, was that she had to keep hemming them.

Leaning against the bedroom door, she listened as her parents' friends laughed and talked in the next room. In all the rooms, really; they spilled into the backyard, and some of them were no doubt wading in the bay.

Basting quick stitches, Kate bit the thread to cut it off. Pinning the needle into her cuff, she pulled the trousers on quickly. Stuffing linen shirttails into them, she glanced at the light spilling through the crack in the door. Her fingers flew along the buttons, then she cinched everything with a fine leather belt.

Heart pounding, she listened again. She had to figure out where her parents were so she could slip out around them. Tinny music bleated from the Victrola, which blended perfectly with glasses clinking. Knotting a tie at her throat, Kate squinted, as if that might help her hear a little better.

"Always sorry to see the fair close," a woman said.

Another woman replied with a snort, "Well, there's the *War* Exposition."

A burst of laughter from the room drowned those voices out. Pulling on a jacket, Kate smoothed herself out and then reached for her hat. She'd already tied her hair in a loose knot on top of her head, and the hat fit neatly over it.

That was the perfect touch; she was transformed. A quick look in the mirror confirmed it: lovely Kate Witherspoon had become a nattily dressed young man.

Slipping her big, boxy camera into a satchel, she took care to fold the crank down and to cover the lens. Then she walked into the party as if she belonged there.

Technically, she did. She was her parents' crowning achievement: a worldly girl who spoke English with an unnamable accent. Her dark eyes and full lips had already inspired any number of paintings, and once, a stained glass window. She could debate the relative merits of the Italian Masters versus the Dutch Masters, grind pigments in her sleep, and had very rarely had the same address for more than a year or two.

Her schooling had been in traveling, learning to read with authors, studying geography by walking it. All of it, always, within arm's reach of her parents. Her sickeningly almost-famous parents, known in "the right circles" and absolutely anonymous out of them. To that wide and limited world, she wasn't Kate Witherspoon. She was *Nathaniel and Amelia's daughter.*

It's not that Kate wanted an ordinary life. She wanted a life of her *own.*

Walking purposefully, she made straight for the door. A certain thrill quivered in her belly as she moved unrecognized among familiar faces. She had a far better method of escape at the ready, but traipsing out before their very eyes delighted her.

Someone dropped the needle on a new record, and everyone shivered with the racing beat. In the corner, Amelia threw her head back in laugher; that sound carried over the noise of the party. Hurrying, Kate darted around a clutch of painters arguing about gouache.

Music trailed after her, even after she slipped outside and down the drive.

The night smelled of jasmine and motor oil as Kate hopped a streetcar at the corner. Paying her fare, she hung off the back rail like the other boys did, careful to hold on to her hat and satchel. Tipping her face to the wind, she savored the rattle of the car beneath her feet and the vastness of the city at night.

If only her camera could capture the stars. Or moonlight

on the waves. Images blossomed in her mind: a lone boat on the horizon, swallowed by the night as constellations drifted in endless loops overhead. At least that idea came in black and white. If she could figure out how to shoot the dark, her father couldn't argue that she wasn't capturing the truth.

When the car slowed near San Diego's Balboa Park, Kate leapt from the platform. The Palais de Danse stood in the distance. Lights gleamed on its whitewashed entrance; its plaster spires curled toward the sky. It looked vaguely Moroccan as long as you'd never been to Marrakesh.

Music poured from the crowded front door. The bright tease of a cornet cut the air, a clarinet squealing along with a piano. Drums and trombone competed in the luscious low notes. The syncopated beat slipped across Kate's skin, tightening her flesh with anticipation.

"One thin dime, fella," the doorman said. "Ladies for free; you got a girl with ya?"

"Not tonight," Kate said, fishing change from her pocket. With a wink, she gave up the dime and elbowed the doorman as she passed. "Maybe I'll get lucky."

He laughed. "That's the spirit!"

Inside, bare bulbs hung from the rafters, a field of manmade stars lighting the dancehall. Humid air pressed all around, ripe with the scent of sweat and perfume. Boys in uniform swirled by, mixed with the ones not yet old enough to head *over there*. Girls with giddy smiles and thin skirts that clung to their thighs danced together, waiting to catch someone's eye.

Kate crammed herself into a corner table, then pulled her camera from the bag. She needed the table to stay steady, since it was impossible to sneak anywhere with a tripod. Tilting the lens toward the ceiling, she counted along with the "Dixie Jass Band One Step" and started to crank.

Jazz and ragtime were perfect for making movies. She had to turn the film at a steady rate or everyone on the reel would look like mad hornets. Speeding up suddenly, dripping down slow like molasses — there was an *art* to capturing moving pictures, no matter what Daddy said.

Taking in the lights first, Kate slowly lowered the camera to capture the people around her. A knot of boys in the corner looked like skinned rabbits in their brand-new military cuts. They passed a wrinkled stub of a cigarette around as they watched the girls moving on the floor.

One of them leaned against his buddy. He gestured subtly, smoke ringing the tips of his fingers. He wasn't looking at the fresh, pretty faces blooming around him. His eyes canted significantly lower; the curve of his smile was dark and a little wild.

Careful to keep her count, Kate filmed every bit of it, even the way he smoothed a sweet mask over his face when a girl would look his way. Kate was capturing magic: the moment between bad intent and good behavior. Moving a bit closer, she reveled; this was perfect for her one-reel.

Threading through the bank of tables, she shifted to catch the other half of that equation. Two girls with their backs to the room threw furtive glances as they shared a pot of lip rouge. Animated as they spoke, one girl was all sharp angles and emphasis. The other nodded, brows rounded earnestly as she listened.

Then the music shifted to a rag, and the girls transformed. Sharp put on a doe-eyed expression, and Rounded turned into something smoky-eyed and assured. Daringly, they arranged themselves right at the edge of the dance floor, and they didn't pretend to be dainty. They caught the soldiers' eyes and danced away in their arms.

"Perfect," Kate murmured to herself, then yelped when someone touched her sleeve.

"Ooh, sorry," a pretty girl in beaded silk said, leaning back. "I didn't mean to sneak up on you."

Kate folded the crank down; no point wasting expensive film on nothing. "It's all right. It's a bit loud in here, don't you think?"

"It is! And quite acoustic! You can stand anywhere at all and hear the music."

"Are you here with friends?" Kate asked. She skimmed

the nearby faces, but everyone savored their own moment, too busy to pay attention to anyone else's.

"Just one. She's already dancing." Seemingly caught on a breath, the girl edged closer. Pulling her gaze back to Kate's face, she smiled again. "With one of the conscripts. Have you filled out your card yet?"

Without hesitation, Kate shook her head. She'd been sneaking out for months now in her father's clothes; most people thought she was barely out of short pants, but so far, no one had realized she wasn't a boy. She'd answered questions about the draft so often, she already had an excuse for her lack of service. "I'm not fit. Curvature of the spine."

"That's too bad; you poor thing."

"I do my best from home," Kate said. With a nod toward the coat check, she said, "How about you wait right here a minute, and then we'll go for a drag?"

The girl finally let out her breath. "Aren't you a sweetheart? I'd love to."

Kate held up one finger, then bounded to the coat check. It cost another dime to leave her camera, but she could be sure that it would be there at the end of the night. Once she gave over to dancing, there was no telling how long the night would be.

Coming back to reclaim her, Kate tugged the girl onto the floor. "So, what's your name?"

"Mollie Foster," she said. "What about you?"

Kate took her hand and twirled her, pulling her back in with a grin. "You wouldn't believe me if I told you."

"Mystery man, all right then." Mollie caught her lip between her teeth, following Kate through a quickstep with ease. "Then . . . maybe you can tell me what you were doing with that box when I interrupted you?"

Shifting with a few skipping steps, Kate smiled. "Making a motion picture."

"You weren't!"

"I was." Kate almost lost her hat when she dipped Mollie. "I'm heading to Hollywood soon. I'm going to show my reel to Biograph. Before you know it, you'll be paying quarters to see my movies."

Mollie considered this a moment, then pressed closer. "People say I look like Mary Pickford."

Rosebud mouth, big blue eyes, coppery curls that caught the light when they bounced — she did look a bit like Pickford, Kate had to admit.

Suddenly, Mollie threw her head back and put on a wide-eyed, innocent expression. Fluttering with a sweet smile, she looked aside, bashful. Then she clasped her hands and peered around anxiously. The music played on behind her, bright in contrast to her pretended fear.

Slowly, Kate smiled. She had plenty of scenery on her

reel. Loads of dancehalls, people swarming on streetcars, and of course, her parents' parties. Those were worth a documentary all their own — the secret lives of expatriates and artists. But what she didn't have, until that very minute, was a star.

Leaning in, Kate whispered, "Can you keep a secret?"

***

The Walk of a Thousand Lights was Los Angeles' finest achievement to date, aside from building a city in the desert. The boardwalk at Long Beach was the Coney Island of the West, a marvel of diversions and technology.

Rifling through a bag of saltwater taffy, a man who called himself Virgil Walker wandered through its crowds. If he noticed the marvels, it was only to squint at them.

Virgil didn't fit in, threading through teen-agers with bright eyes and a little spending money at hand. Worn with the years, Virgil's boots were old, but his jacket new, and the haircut was the first he'd had in quite some time.

He moved deliberately, assaulted by the scents, the sounds. The boardwalk was lit like day, roaring with laughter and conversation. Screams rang out, measured by the clatter of a wooden roller coaster.

From all sides, the ocean beckoned — casting cold mist into the air. Concession carts offered roasted nuts and candy floss; a pretty girl in red flirted passing sailors into buying bottles of Coca-Cola. A barker leaned into Virgil's path, trying to lure him closer.

"Guess your weight, sir, step right up, win a prize!"

Virgil waved him off and popped another piece of taffy into his mouth. The sweetness spread on his tongue, thick like honey. It covered his sour breath, and it felt like eating something substantial. He had nothing in his pockets but a tattered map and a ticket for the red streetcars.

Looping around the carousel, Virgil stopped to orient himself. The manager's office was supposed to be right there. He turned, trying not to get swept up in the current of the crowd. It was too many people, too much noise. Squaring his shoulders, he waded toward the shadowy storefronts behind the carts.

"Nothing to see back there," a vendor said, catching Virgil's arm.

With a jerk, Virgil rubbed his sleeve hard. "Where's the midway office?"

The vendor nodded his head. "Other side, pal."

Back into the throng of bodies, Virgil ignored the way his skin crawled. He'd spent too many years on the sea; walking on the ground felt like stomping rocks. He couldn't get used to seeing faces and buildings and wires instead of miles off to the horizon.

But he needed a job. Hopefully something out of the crowds. Handing out towels at the bathhouse, or cleaning up after everybody went home. He was so focused on the office door that he didn't see the belled and beaded fortune teller step into his path.

"My mystic eye — " she began.

Hissing curses, Virgil shoved her to the ground. Snatching the turban from the fortune teller's head, he loomed over her. Red and orange silk unfurled, a bright flag in his hands. Snapping the fabric tight, Virgil bent down, his face contorted to a vicious mask.

A sailor grabbed him by the neck. Two others hurried to help the fortune teller to her feet. Silver bells jingled violently. Ducking under the sailor's hand, Virgil leveled him with two sharp blows to the kidneys.

For a moment, all had been silence. Now the crowd swarmed. They buzzed with blood and fury; he couldn't win. Flinging the turban down, Virgil took off. He crashed into hard shoulders and soft bodies. A cry went up the boardwalk as he tore through the crowds.

Soon, he was far enough away to stop, to slip between buildings to catch his breath.

Bile rose in his throat, and he sucked blood from his lip. Still trembling with adrenaline, he slid down the wall. His black eyes cut toward the sky, toward familiar stars that never led him home. The man who called himself Virgil Walker sat in the alley and *remembered*.

Once, his name had been Caleb Grey. He'd lived in Baltimore by the sea and loved a girl who bore a bow like Artemis. She'd tasted of caramel and salt and pleasure; she was going to be his wife. Then Amelia van den Broek had lied to him, laughed at him, and stolen his true love away.

Once, his name had been Caleb Grey, but not now and never again. He couldn't go home. His Sarah was dead.

And that fortune-telling bitch had never paid.

Four

Sneaking back into the house was a little trickier with a friend in tow. Kate and Mollie stood on the corner, the last stop of the night for the streetcar. A chill hung in the air, laced with fog. It swirled at their feet as they walked through it, arm in arm.

"Which house is yours?" Mollie asked.

Vaguely embarrassed, Kate raised one hand and pointed. It was the house with all the lights on, of course, with music still playing. Most of the beachcombers had gone back inside, which meant even more people to avoid.

Mollie whistled low. "Wow. They really *are* party fiends."

"I told you." Kate sighed. "All right, come on. We'll go to the back door, and we'll have thirty seconds. Take the hallway left, then the first right, then the first door on the left."

Giggles rolled from Mollie's lips. "They don't seem like fuddy-duddies. Why all the sneaking?"

"This is my father's suit," Kate explained. "He doesn't exactly approve."

"Ohhh."

Kate took Mollie's hand and led her along the side of the house. The stucco plucked at their clothes, pulling Mollie's hair and clinging to Kate's hat. They dipped beneath the kitchen window, which was thrown open to let in the air and let out the scent of smoke and sweat.

Creeping along, Kate felt for the door. On the other side, a black, caged bird flapped its wings and croaked at them. Pressing a finger to her lips, Kate shushed it.

Then she caught Mollie's hand and pressed herself against the wall. Sneaking past the party had been easy; she'd need her gift to get back in with Mollie in tow. Exhaling, Kate drained herself until a familiar spark glowed at the edge of her sight. Seconds ticked by, her sight growing dimmer. Her ears rang, a high-pitched chime only she could hear. When the shadows threatened to swallow her, a thread of orange light streaked by.

It felt like the world turning under her feet, and when she blinked, she saw a glimpse of that boy, always that boy, handsome with his brown eyes and golden hair. For the longest time, he'd seemed much older . . . but suddenly, Kate felt a whisper on her skin, a touch of realization — they were the same age now. A fluttered urgency filled her, but when she reached for him, the vision popped like a bubble.

Struck by the high drama of sneaking in, Mollie clapped a hand over her mouth to keep from laughing aloud. But then her smile faltered, because suddenly it was silent. It was like someone had dropped a bowl on top of the party. The music stopped; glasses stilled. Mollie couldn't help but notice that no one moved.

The guests stood frozen with drinks halfway to their mouths. Cigarette smoke hung from some lips, apparitions fixed in hazy place. Mollie stared at a dancing woman, head thrown back and caught in a spin. Casually defying gravity, the beads on her dress stood out like spines.

"Hurry," Kate said, tugging her hand. "It won't last."

Scrambling after her, Mollie tried to find words, but there were none. She'd seen an impossible thing; her thoughts were as frozen as the revelers. Except, the moment Kate closed her bedroom door, it all roared to motion again. The rush of sound after silence was almost deafening, and Mollie put her hands over her ears.

"What . . . what was that?"

Kate opened her armoire, stripping the suit off as quickly as she could. "It's just a thing I can do. It doesn't matter."

Speechless once more, Mollie opened the door a crack to peer out. There were no statues or stilled smoke now. Everything, everyone, moved once more. It really had been an impossible thing. Before she could convince herself she'd imagined it all, a woman strode down the hall.

Suddenly Mollie whispered, "Somebody's coming."

With a hiss, Kate peeled herself down to her silk combination, then kicked the suit under the bed. Grabbing her robe, Kate threw it on quickly. Mollie plucked the hat from Kate's head and tossed it into the corner.

A gentle knock sounded on the door. "Kate?"

Yanking the pin out of her hair, Kate tossed it to the floor. Feigning a yawn, Kate said, "Mimi?"

Unimpressed with Kate's performance, Amelia crossed her arms. Her dark eyes trailed over Kate's face, studying her and all her minute details. Finally reaching out, she touched the robe's collar and asked, "Inside out, mm?"

"I was sleeping. I put it on in the dark," Kate said smartly.

Pursing her lips, Amelia pushed the door open a little more. "I doubt that. Your father and I felt you come in."

"If you already know, why ask?"

"You smell like gin."

"Gin doesn't smell like anything," Kate replied. "And I wasn't drinking. I was dancing."

Even if Kate had wanted to look contrite, she simply couldn't manage the expression. Her parents were proud and independent — they lived without an address, refused to marry, and acknowledged no higher power but art. They should have expected their only child to be just like them.

"You know, you have a remarkable amount of freedom. If you'd asked . . ."

"I didn't want to ask!"

Amelia sighed and leaned against the frame of the door. Delicate lines traced the corners of her eyes. A certain sharpness had replaced the youthful curve of her cheeks. Her face was a mirror of the future; Kate could see herself in it easily.

"Is someone in there with you?"

Revealing the answer with a glance, Kate nodded. "I've found my star. The world is going to fall in love with her."

Voice soft, Amelia spoke into the room. "Hello, star."

Hesitant, Mollie pressed her back against the wall. But when Kate held out a hand, she slowly melted into view. Her cheeks were stained pink, and she struggled to meet Amelia's gaze. "I'm not trying to cause a fuss. I just want to be in pictures, ma'am."

"Where are your parents?"

"I haven't got any," Mollie said. "I live at the Women and Children's Home. Well, I did. I'm old enough to make my own way now."

"See?" Kate asked. "She hasn't anywhere to go."

"I've been sleeping on the beach," Mollie admitted.

Kate watched her mother's expression go distant. It always did when she talked to her father in their intimate, soundless way. Then, at once, her gaze sharpened, present once more in the moment. "What's your name?"

"Mollie Foster," she said, her spine going straight.

"She's going to be bigger than Pearl White," Kate interrupted. "People will forget all about *The Perils of Pauline* when they see Mollie on-screen."

Patiently, Amelia waited for Kate to quiet, then said, "All right, then. She'll be staying."

Kate looked to Mollie, then back to her mother. "Do you mean it?"

"We're not leaving San Diego yet," Amelia said, stepping back into the hall. "And we have plenty of room. I'm not turning a child loose on the beach at this hour."

Throwing herself into Amelia's arms, Kate hugged her fiercely. They were exactly the same height. "Oh, you're my favorite, Mimi. Thank you!"

Chiming in, Mollie beamed. "Thank you, ma'am."

A grimace touched Amelia's brow, but she smoothed it away with her fingertips. "Give her one of your nightgowns, Kate. And both of you get to bed."

Pressing a kiss to Kate's forehead, then shaking Mollie's hand, Amelia excused herself and returned to the party.

Kate closed the door and exclaimed, "I can't believe they're letting you stay. But, oh, they had to! I would have insisted."

"Can I tell you a secret?" Mollie asked.

Kate opened her armoire, rummaging for two gowns. Possibility danced through her thoughts, and she could hardly keep from smiling. She'd never had a friend to stay. Sometimes, when she was little, her parents would have friends with children over, but that was hardly the same as picking a confederate of her own. To have someone to share secrets, to make plans with — it was unbearably wonderful. "Tell me anything."

Mollie said, "None of that was true."

Butterflies fluttered in Kate's stomach. Turning to look at her, she asked, "What do you mean?"

Mollie dropped herself onto the foot of Kate's bed, then fell back among the pillows. Spicy perfume wafted up, a dot of it on the sheets always to sweeten the room. Kicking up her feet, she stroked her fingers along the fine linens. Finally, she tipped her head to catch Kate's eye.

"My father lives in Old Town. He's a street sweeper."

"What?"

Mollie went on. "I've slept on the beach once or twice, but only because I wanted to."

A glittering chill swept over Kate's skin. "You were . . . you were lying?"

"No," Mollie said. She lifted her head, curls cascading from her shoulders, a victorious smile touching the corners of her lips. "I was *acting*."

Wringing a nightgown into a knot, Kate stood silently for a moment. No clock ticked, but the relative quiet seemed to count itself, stretching out in waves. Then, with two running steps, Kate leapt onto the bed, planting her feet next to Mollie's head. Too giddy to hold still, she bounced.

"That was amazing," she said.

Mollie laughed, reaching for the nightgown. "Do I get the part?"

All Kate could see were the flickering lights of the theatre and the way she'd frame Mollie's face with the camera. Theda Bara had nothing but smoky looks to recommend her; Pickford played the same role again and again. People would line up for days! Riot in the streets! Beg on the corners and pay twice the price to get a glimpse at the latest Witherspoon and Foster reel!

Looking down at her star, Kate swore, "All of them. Every single one."

<hr />

Sam led the way through the darkened wood. The moonlight was so bright that he and Julian cast shadows. A choir of crickets keened, stopping abruptly when Sam kicked a stone out of the way.

"Probably our last boys' night," he told Julian.

"Will you stop saying that?" Julian prodded his brother with the foot of his crutch, then hurried to keep his pace. "You sound like a doom clock. The end is near! The end is near!"

Sam swooped down and rose again with a branch in one hand. "Maybe I know something you don't know."

Prodding him again, Julian snorted. "Do you? Do you really, Sam? Hey, maybe pigs fly!"

"Mmm, wingèd bacon. Floats right into your mouth."

"Better shut up before they ration that, too."

They both laughed, continuing their march through the dark. At the other end of the path, Charlie and Henry had already built a fire. Root beer chilled in a basket in the creek. There was a good chance they'd share if the younger brothers managed to wrestle the bottle opener from them.

Charlie called out when he saw Sam and Julian emerge from the woods. "What's the password?"

"Chucks!" Sam called back.

"Sorry," Henry said, dipping a twig into the flames and shaking his head. "Try again."

Heading for the fire, Julian said, "I know what you did with Papa's binoculars."

Charlie whistled, circling away from him. "Straight for the blackmail."

"I told you Julian was the evil one." Henry grinned, swirling the burning twig in the air. He drew his name and a star, then tossed the stick back into the fire.

With two more steps, Charlie crashed into Sam. Slinging an arm around his neck, he ground his knuckles against his head. Built solidly, the tallest of all of them, Charlie barely moved as Sam struggled to escape. "What about you, jack-a-dandy?"

"Your mother's a pork pie!"

Henry jumped in then, which left Julian to sneak into the root beers early. Popping the top, he caught the foam as it spilled over the mouth of the bottle. That was the best part of any beer: its flavor distilled into effervescence.

By the time the rest of his brothers came up for air, Julian had finished half a bottle, nailed the cap into the side of his stump-chair, and settled in by the fire. Gentle waves of heat washed his skin. Embers circled toward the stars, lightning bugs flashing along the lawn.

This was a fine place, Charlie and Henry's cottage at the far side of the farm.

After staggering in, Sam flopped onto the ground. He tugged Henry's pantleg. "Bring me a root beer?"

"Nope," Henry said, but fetched the basket anyway.

Charlie took the stump closest to Julian. Always fussing, he moved Julian's crutches back from the fire and kicked his foot a little. Charlie shrugged apologetically. "I'll catch hell if you get burned."

Rolling his eyes, Julian moved a fraction of an inch, then gave Charlie a warning look. That was all the fretting he planned to put up with tonight.

Still, Julian felt the slightest bit guilty, because Charlie had always been better than a brother. The first raspberries of the season were always his because Charlie brought them up from the riverbank for him. When they both still went to school, Charlie pulled him in a wagon so he wouldn't have to walk the three miles into town.

Raising his bottle, Julian nudged him. "Hope you got me something good for my birthday."

Serious, Charlie said, "I'm getting engaged."

"Told you," Sam whispered near Julian's ear.

Henry nearly fell into the fire. "How come I'm just now finding out?"

He and Charlie had built the cottage together, moving into it the minute Henry turned eighteen. Though they worked the family farm, they had a little slice of independence at the end of the day. They were a team; at least, they always had been.

Sam hummed a funeral dirge, and Julian said, "You sure don't sound happy about it."

"I got called up." Pulling an envelope from his back pocket, he waved it listlessly. There was no missing the War Department's seal on the return address. "It's not right to make Marjorie wait 'til I get back. Mama's been saying she could use some help in the house, so I expect Marjorie'll move in . . ."

Pushing a hand into his hair, Henry sat back hard. "I don't know what to say."

"It was bound to happen." Charlie turned the envelope in his fingers, over and over, as if it might change shape or fly away. He had strong hands — broad fingers and wide palms. But they were gentle, and it was hard to imagine them holding a rifle.

"Well." Sam flipped a bottle cap into the fire, then looked up. "Can I move in here, then?"

Julian shoved him off the stump, and Henry tossed his hat after him. Charlie didn't bother to intervene. He stared into the flames, his eyes reflecting shadows from the inside, and the out.

Clapping a hand on Charlie's shoulder, Julian waited for him to look over. "It'll be all right. Papa said it's about over but for the crying."

With a trace of a smile, Charlie cracked his knuckles. "I hope he's right."

After that, they were quiet. Lips on bottles and a crackling fire joined the frogs and crickets, but the Birch brothers ruminated instead.

Julian ached. He'd read so many accounts of mustard gas attacks that he'd had nightmares about it. Men trapped in trenches, poison rolling over them . . . It made Julian sick to think of Charlie out there among them.

Sam rose to his feet. "All right, girls, quit your bellyaching."

Henry scowled. "I hope Mama hears you say that."

Sam ignored him, turning to Julian. His bright eyes shone as he clapped his hands, as if warming up to something. There was an air of carnival barker to him, that same big, bright personality that drove girls mad and drove his brothers to distraction. "Julie, do your trick for us."

Incredulous, Julian stared at him. "You go take a leap."

Charlie cleared his throat. Rubbing his hands together, he still gazed into the fire, but he said, "I could stand to see it again."

Since Charlie wanted it, it would happen. Like that, Sam and Henry went to work looking for suitable subjects. Julian watched them, darting into the cottage and out, turning over stones and peering under the porch. It only took a few minutes for them to return to the circle.

Henry stood back as Sam thrust a rusty pie tin into Julian's lap. Somehow, those mad beasts had found three beetles, a lightning bug, and a salamander — all dead.

Sliding to the ground, Julian leaned against the stump. Slowly, he raised the tin to eye level. When he drew his next breath, he tasted dust and ash. Inhaling until his lungs burned, Julian courted an uncertain sensation. It felt like his tether to the earth might slip; he was a balloon dancing on a string. Then, at once, he blew across the still bodies in the tin.

One by one, they flickered to life. Tiny legs trembled, and the beetles flipped themselves over. Even in this faint light, their iridescent shells shimmered. With a rattle, they spread their wings and flew off.

A faint glow signaled the lightning bug's return. As it

staggered along the plate, its flashes coming brighter and faster, the salamander opened its eyes. Wary, it blinked and breathed but refused to move. Sam touched its tail, but it clung to the illusion of death.

"Take it," Julian said, shoving the plate into Charlie's hands. The wave was coming. He steeled himself, then slumped into darkness. Perfect night consumed him — no light, no stars. No sound, no breath. Nothing, he was simply nothing, forever, and for a moment.

Suddenly, a streak of sunset spread in the distance. The girl turned again, her hair flowing like water. It was black but for a lone wave of silver that threaded itself among the rest. She was a siren; her gaze slipped right into him.

For the first time, he saw her details; he tasted honeysuckle on the wind. Since the very first time Julian had used his gift, she'd been waiting for him. Now he had the reeling sensation that she was alive; real — truly waiting for him. She reached for him —

And then he opened his eyes. For a split second, Julian felt every part of his body waking. It was like a machineworks grinding back to motion. Blood pounded in his ears, every hair prickled. Muscles burned and learned to stretch again. It was pain and pleasure at once, one overwhelming moment of awareness.

He was alive, he breathed — from his brothers' perspective, he'd simply dropped his head and then raised it again.

Whooping, Sam stepped over the fire, celebrating, and Henry carried the salamander back to the woodpile. But Charlie smoothed Julian's hair back. He studied him with gentle eyes, a shadow cut into his brow.

With a shake, Charlie asked, "All right?"

Hoping his big brother had seen what he needed to, Julian simply nodded.

<center>~~~~~~~</center>

Nathaniel leaned against the wall, gazing out the window. The first shades of dawn weren't on them yet, but their guests had tottered home. It was a chance to listen to the house settle. To the sea in the distance. To the wear of Amelia's feet across the thick Persian rug.

"Why don't you let me rub your neck?" he asked, following the ghost of Amelia's image in the glass.

"I don't understand her, Nate," Amelia replied. Her silken dressing gown puffed like a sail when she threw up her hands. "I have no idea what would make her happy."

Lips barely moving, Nathaniel said, "I don't know that you're supposed to."

Amelia narrowed her eyes at him. "Oh, such composure. As if you weren't apoplectic when you caught her kissing that boy in Paris."

"That jackal, you mean."

"I said what I meant. I always do."

She dared him to argue, then stood. Drifting back to him, she slipped her arms round his waist. Pressed her cheek to his shoulder. The familiar warmth of his skin soothed her.

"Amelia," he murmured, covering her arms with his own.

Melting against his back, Amelia sighed. "I'm waiting for the inevitable disaster."

That truth, finally spoken, hung heavy between them. Turning in her arms, Nathaniel rested his brow against hers. His fingertips walked her back, trailing up into the tangle of her hair. "Did you see something?"

The moment he asked, he wished the question back. The last time Amelia had peeked at the future, it was 1889, and thereafter, everything went to pieces. That summer had burned her so completely, she hadn't looked since — no matter how tempting.

Amelia said, "No, I lived it."

"Of course you did. Didn't we all?"

She kissed him, and lips still clinging, she whispered on his mouth, "Take me somewhere."

Folding around her, Nathaniel pulled them into the wind.

It had grown easier over the years. Once, he'd had to *will* the elements to part for him. There was force to it. A certain sharp-toothed deliberation.

Now, over continents and decades, carrying Amelia and Kate, it took nothing at all to move them. In fact, sometimes it seemed harder for him to stay in place.

When the dark parted around them, they stood on the balcony of a tower. Robe billowing, Amelia closed her eyes and leaned into the wind. It was cooler here, and it carried the perfume of warm figs.

"Better?" Nathaniel asked.

She nodded, fingers curled around the wrought-iron rail. As her hair pulled free, she shook it from her face, staring resolutely into the distance. "I always thought if we made sure she saw everything, experienced everything . . ."

With a sideward glance, Nathaniel said, "Then what?"

Frustrated, she threw up her hands. "I don't know, Nate. I don't know. Happily ever after? Nothing would ever go wrong again? I don't know."

"What can she possibly do with an extra thirty seconds that she couldn't do without it?" It was the first time he'd asked the question aloud. Until then, it had been a private shield, a perfect curve of steel to keep him from wondering too much, worrying too much.

Turning to Nathaniel, Amelia curled her fingers round

his wrist, counting the beats of his heart. "In the beginning, I saw a single vision at a time. Look what became of it."

Nathaniel pursed his lips, then after a moment said, "Do you know what I think?"

"Far too often, but please, do go ahead."

"If she were the very same girl that she is at this moment, but stripped of her silver hair and ability to stop time" — he squeezed Amelia's arms gently — "we'd still be having this conversation."

A soft sigh on her lips, Amelia rested against his shoulder once more. Exhaustion rippled through her. It had been a long night: too many people, too many emotions.

Weary, she closed her eyes and asked, "Why are you such a monster?"

Nathaniel kissed her brow and gathered her again. Holding the wind off long enough to reply, he filled her ears with the low, dark honey of his voice and the only answer he ever gave: "How else would you have me?"

Five

The next evening came, and hurricane lamps cast a warm glow across the Birches' backyard. Sweet hickory smoke wound toward a cloudless sky, and Zora carried a pitcher of mint lemonade from the kitchen.

Adding it to an already laden table, Zora laughed when Emerson abandoned his grill to pick her up. He spun her gently, flashes of calico and lace swirling, then dropped her back to her feet. Beckoned by the curve of her neck, he answered with one kiss, and then two.

"I wonder who that is," Zora said, catching his arm and holding him in place. "I hope it's my husband."

"Were you expecting him, ma'am?" Emerson asked.

Laughing, Zora nudged him with her shoulder. Then she

settled beneath the sheltering curve of his body. He smelled of smoke and sweat, and beneath that, clean, new earth. She swayed with him, smiling at the party that sprawled across her lawn.

Sam stood on his hands, showing off for a cloud of pretty, perfumed girls from town. From his sprawl on a bench, Henry picked through a bowl of ambrosia salad as he talked with one of the Hawkins boys.

Brow furrowing, Zora asked, "Do you see Julian?"

Emerson kissed her neck again. "Nope."

Amused, Zora rephrased her question. "Do you know where Julian is?"

"Yep."

"Em," Zora said, and slipped out of his arms. She backed away from him, plucking up a pair of salad tongs to brandish. He straightened to his full height, then took a step toward her. Warning, Zora repeated, "Em!"

"Zo," he replied. His boot fell heavy on the porch, another stride closer.

Drawing herself up imperiously, Zora said, "Emerson Birch, where is our youngest child?"

At once, Emerson stopped. His whole posture changed, lanky and gentle again as he reached for her. "Oh, Julian? He's in the barn."

Exasperated, Zora asked, "You couldn't have told me that in the first place?"

"No, ma'am."

"And why not?"

Emerson caught her hand and closed the space between them. Backing her toward the porch rail, he smiled as he leaned down to whisper against her cheek. "Because he's in there with a girl."

"Elise?" Zora leaned her head back, her pale eyes sparkling. "How long have they been in there? Maybe I should bring them some cake."

Looping an arm around Zora's waist, Emerson twirled her slowly, lazily, and said, "Maybe you should leave them alone and dance with me."

"But there's no music."

"I'll sing some for you," he replied.

Stepping into a waltz with him, Zora's heart fluttered when he made good on that promise. His smooth tenor notes seemed to slip right under her skin; his familiar hands became brand-new on her as they turned and turned in the shadows of the porch.

Glancing up, she caught him in her gaze. There was always something to find in his eyes — unexpected wildness, or teasing, or in that very moment, longing. Old infatuation raced through her skin. She felt light and beautiful and invincible.

Emerson let the song trail off, murmuring a quiet confession. "I love dancing with you."

In spite of the blush stinging her cheeks, Zora pressed a finger to his lips. "Shhh. I can't hear the music."

"What's that?" he asked, lifting her again. "I can't hear you over the music."

They laughed together and took a few more steps. There was still a cake to serve and ice cream to scoop, and a few small presents to give to the birthday boy to open. With a gentle kiss, Zora finally stepped back. But her touch lingered.

Holding Emerson's hand for a moment more, she said, "Things are good, aren't they?"

"Yes ma'am" He kissed her fingertips and smiled against them. "They always are."

Down by the water, Mollie stood framed in a sandstone arch. Pinned into a vaguely medieval dress, and crowned with a band of paper and foil, she shivered. The sea wind streamed around her, pulling her hair and her hems.

"Do we have enough light?" she asked.

She hadn't complained all afternoon. Not when they'd had to flee when sea lions took over the beach. Nor when Kate asked her to lie down and let the surf wash over her. But the light was fading; the pleasant afternoon promised to be a chilly evening, and Mollie was still damp.

Kate moved her tripod again. Though sand was a good base for it, the ground wasn't level. She couldn't afford to waste film, so everything had to be right. She glanced at the sky and sighed. Blue shifted toward slate gray in the east. Sunset threatened to be ordinary, a few plum-tinged clouds loitering above a hazy sea.

A porcelain rattle interrupted Kate's geometry. Raising her head from her camera, she saw Mollie clamp her mouth shut to try to stop the chattering of her teeth.

Though she hated to admit it, Kate was somewhat torn. Guilt roiled in her belly, but her gaze sharpened. She couldn't help but notice that Mollie suffered beautifully.

She looked every inch the miserable Lady of Shalott. Her longing for . . . well, for dry clothes and a warm meal played out on her delicate features like the raw and unrestrained longing of a maiden cursed to see Lancelot, to love him, but to never have him.

Perhaps a true artist would have ignored her muse's torment. But, since Mollie was the first friend Kate had had, and she rather wanted to keep her, she abandoned art for the day. Covering the lens on her camera, she beckoned to her. "We can come back."

Throwing her arms around herself, Mollie huddled against the stone wall until Kate finished packing her gear. Then she darted up to her, skirts bunched in one hand. Painting herself against Kate's side, she wanted to say something, but her teeth clattered violently instead. That set her to giggling, and Kate wrapped an arm around her to share her warmth.

"Perhaps tomorrow," Kate said, hustling her toward home. "We should build a fire to keep you warm between takes."

Mollie lit up. "Oh, let's. We could bring potatoes to put in the embers. I adore a roast potato. When the skin is all crispy and lovely . . ."

"We need to find a canoe," Kate replied, distracted. Mollie was a stunning Lady of Shalott, but they needed a boat for her to die in, and a Lancelot to die for.

There were so many things to manage, so many details to cover. Plotting the final reel, imagining it in all its glory, consumed every stray thought in Kate's head.

With a little pinch to catch Kate's attention, Mollie said, "We'll find one. Stop worrying."

"It's not worrying," Kate said. "I'm managing the production. That's how films get made, you know. Careful steward-ship, a keen eye for accounting, a knack for solving sticky staging dilemmas . . ."

At that, Mollie dropped her head and pretended to snore.

Kate pinched her back and laughed when she bolted away from Mollie. Calling to her, Kate said, "Someone has to mind the details!"

Hurrying up the cliff walk, they cut through dune grass, ignoring the way it bit their ankles, because that was the shortest path. The house was a rich, amber jewel set among a jade field of sand verbena and Torrey pines.

Lights flickered in a few of the windows, chasing away night before it had even come. There were no automobiles in the yard today; no music drifted from the open windows. Mollie disappeared down the hall to change before Kate even reached the door.

The candied richness of sautéed onions wafted over her when she walked in. Her father stood at the stove, survey-ing his kingdom of pots and pans. Holding a wooden spoon aloft, he didn't raise his head when he said, "Good day?"

Circumspect, Kate put her tripod against the pantry. "Yes, it was very clear."

"What are you working on?"

Now suspicious, Kate studied him. He was in shirtsleeves

and spattered with paint, the same as he always was. A smudge from Mimi's charcoals darkened his cheek. Everything about him seemed ordinary and usual, including the question that had no right answer.

So long as Kate worked on motion pictures instead of dead, dull gouaches, he would find her art lacking.

Pulling her leather satchel off, Kate said, "An adaptation of a Tennyson poem."

"Oh, Tennyson?"

And there it was. "It has nothing to do with the Pre-Raphaelites, Daddy!"

Tension rippled briefly across his face, but when he spoke, he measured his words. Slipping the towel from his shoulder, he wrapped his hands in it as he turned to her. "Did I say it did?"

"No, but I know exactly what you're thinking." She counted her reasons out for him. "I've only the one actress and no actors at all. It was *Lady of Shalott* or *La Belle Dame sans Merci.* I can manage the former without an actor better than the latter, that's all!"

Nathaniel pressed his lips together. "There's always Ophelia . . ."

"That's a monologue, Daddy, not a — "

A shriek cut them off. Forgetting their quarrel, they

hurried toward the back of the house, where another scream erupted. Kate's bedroom door was closed, and she pushed herself between it and her father.

"No! She was changing," Kate said, then opened the door enough to slide through the crack.

In a rush, Mollie stumbled toward her. Her tangled curls bounced on her shoulders, and her face had gone entirely ashen. Tripping over clothes discarded on the floor, she all but crashed into Kate. Clinging to her, she whispered, "This house is haunted!"

As that was quite possibly the last thing Kate expected to hear, she shook her head as she set Mollie on her feet again. "No, it's not."

"It is! I tell you, it is!" Mollie jabbed a finger at the back wall, toward the changing screen. "I was down to my combination, and I heard a man say something! I turned around, and there was no one there. So I thought, I must have overheard something from the kitchen. Or perhaps I'm weary from working so hard today . . ."

"You did work hard," Kate agreed, petting her hair.

"But then it happened again! It was awful! He said I was going to die!"

When Mollie said that, Kate dissolved into laughter. She backed toward the open window, hands up as she reassured her. "No, no, I'm not laughing at you, I'm not. But I know what your ghost is."

"Do you?" Mollie asked, brittle.

Kate leaned out the window. "Come on, get down here!"

A great black bird dropped from the eaves of the house to land on Kate's outstretched arm. The creature was massive, bigger than a house cat, and dark as sin. When Kate pulled him inside, she smiled as he nudged his head against her cheek. Her arm bobbed beneath his weight, but she kept him aloft as she carried him toward Mollie.

"This is Handsome, and he doesn't want you to die."

"That's a bird, Kate! Oh, put him back outside!" Mollie kept backing away. "They're dirty!"

Kate stroked her fingers along his velvet feathers. "Oh, not him. Ravens love a bath; at least, Handsome does. He's terribly smart, too. Tell her, darling."

Raising his broad wings, Handsome shook himself out a bit, then turned his head nearly upside down. Keen eyes blinked, and then he opened his beak. An eerie, rattling voice issued from him. "I can talk. Can you fly?"

Mollie slumped against the door. "How on earth . . . ?"

"Isn't he fantastic? He can say a few more things, but he usually doesn't." She laughed when Handsome interrupted her again to ask if she could fly. "Daddy taught him that. He thinks it's absolutely hilarious."

"It's bad luck to have a bird in the house," Mollie said.

Kate made a kissing sound and nuzzled Handsome right back. "I raised him from a chick. He's not bad luck at all."

Unconvinced, Mollie said nothing. She kept Handsome in her sight, creeping around the edge of the room to get back to the dressing screen. When she picked up her dress, Handsome spread his wings and cried out.

Mollie let out another shriek, then one more when Nathaniel rapped on the door and demanded to know what was going on in there. Trying to soothe everyone at once, Kate let herself out and smiled at her father.

"All's well," she sang.

Nathaniel sighed as she walked away, and said, to himself alone, "Of course it is."

~~~~

With a pop and a bite of sulfur, a match sprang to life between Julian's fingers. A single point of fire spread inside the glass walls of the lantern, casting a soft circle of light in the middle of the pole barn.

It revealed a working space with bales of hay stacked in the corners and up in the loft. In the dark, the plow and hay cutter seemed like exotic beasts — the cutter's head a dragon; the plow's handles a bull.

A wooden swing drifted lazily, wide enough for two and dangling from the loft with a pulley at the side.

Hanging the lantern and shaking out the match, Julian turned. Outlined by the golden glow, Elise stood in the middle of the floor, looking toward the ceiling. She'd laced ribbon in her hair, and her earbobs swung as she moved.

"You have mourning doves up there," she said.

Julian rubbed his hands dry on his pants. "They're hiding from the owls."

Gathering her skirt in one hand, Elise moved through the barn as if she'd never seen one. Her fingers trailed the poles, and she stopped to read what the Birch boys had penciled on them over the years.

Suddenly, she burst out laughing. *"C dropped the baby 1900."*

Julian said, "He probably wasn't the only one."

Still giggling, Elise tipped sideways to read another. *"H broken arm 1908."*

Julian sat on the swing and pushed his crutches back into the dark. "He likes to say Sam pushed him out of the hayloft, but it's not true. Old Man Henry lost his balance. Lucky he didn't crack his skull open."

"I don't remember that," Elise said. *"C + S 1910.* That one's in a heart. Was that Sarah?"

Julian shook his head. "A girl from out of town; came out to stay with Mr. and Mrs. Routh a while back. Sofia, I think? Brown hair, done up in a bunch of loopty braids . . ."

Pressing against a pole, Elise laughed. "*Loopty* braids."

"You know what I mean."

"I do. I'm just reeling at your way with words." She cast her gaze toward the loft. There were notes written there, too. "Aren't any of these about you?"

Heart racing, Julian patted the empty space beside him. "Most of mine are up top. Come here, I'll show you."

The mourning doves chirred in the rafters as Elise crossed the floor. It seemed like a faint buzz surrounded her, as if she carried open current on her skin. Pinning her skirts between her knees, she sank down with him and smiled. "Hiding a telescope over here?"

Feeding off that current, Julian grabbed the secondary rope and pulled. With a faint squeak every half turn, the pulley above them rolled, and the swing rose into the air. It was perfect for loading hay into the loft, and for scribing secrets into raw wood.

Julian hauled them up easily, savoring the burn of exertion. There was something primal about proving his strength to Elise. He wanted her to notice the breadth of his shoulders and the certainty in his hands.

They'd grown up together, and he remembered when Elise was nothing but elbows and knees. Whatever memory like that she had of him, he wanted it to burn away for good.

A little below the loft, Julian wound the rope on its hook. He tested the knot, then looked to Elise. "All right?"

Twining her arm around the rope on her side, Elise leaned forward to measure their height. The swing tilted with her, and she laughed in surprise. It sounded delicate and thin, nothing like her usual laugh. "Don't let me fall."

"I wouldn't ever," Julian swore. Then, brazen and brave, and perhaps a little crazy, he slipped an arm around her. His hand fell to her hip; his thumb grazed the curve of her waist. That glancing touch, drawing off her warmth and her softness, intoxicated him.

Elise swallowed a soft sound, craning to look past him and behind herself. "You promised me inscriptions."

"I did, fair enough," he said. His knee brushed hers as he turned the swing. "All the way that way, at the corner. Do you see it? *J can fly 1907*."

"Julian, how did you get that there?"

"I flew!"

With an expectant smile, Elise leveled a gaze at him. She didn't say anything, and she didn't have to. Her quirked eyebrow spoke for her.

"I laid out in the loft. I have a gift for writing upside down," he admitted.

Relaxing, Elise searched for another marking. The thin light danced, revealing and hiding handwriting that went from unsure to confident, growing bolder by the year. Crinkling her nose, she puzzled over another cryptic note. *"J DITV 5-6-1911."*

"The first time my father let me play 'Down in the Valley' on his fiddle after Sunday dinner."

"I do love listening to you on that fiddle," Elise said. She leaned against him, her head brushing his shoulder.

The lantern below was only so bright. It cast its fullest light on the floor and faded to an intimation of illumination above it. Elise and Julian were drawn in stark lines — faint light, but inky shadows. Her soft mouth became lush; her brows arched in pure, clean strokes.

Julian drank in her every detail. But for all his admiration of her clear eyes and the sable wing of her lashes, his gaze ultimately lingered on her lips. She was so close — so warm — he skimmed his thumb against her waist again. Everything inside him tightened, like he was being tuned to her key.

Fingers fluttering against his arm, Elise filled half the space between them. Julian filled the rest, his breath tracing warm against her skin as their lips met. It was barely a caress, more discovery than anything else.

Hanging above the barn floor, the swing drifted a lazy pattern. Nudged one way when Julian finally kissed her, it jolted abruptly when Elise broke away.

The current faltered.

His head still all white noise, Julian stared at her. He had no words in his mouth; everything was a jumble. In retreat, he asked, "What's wrong?"

All the warmth between them drained away. Elise looked at the ceiling, then took a deep breath. Her graceful hands turned fidgety, pulling at the neck of her dress. The pretty cream lace there cast shadowed barbs on her throat.

"Elise, what?"

"I shouldn't have come in here," she said. Her voice wavered, and her lips, so lush with anticipation in the moment past, now trembled. "I'm sorry."

Numb, Julian reached for the pulley rope. With clumsy hands he unmoored them and struggled to lower them to the ground. He wanted to let go, to go crashing down and shatter on the floor.

Doubts and questions careened through him. He bled from the inside, and the only thing he could think of to say was, "I thought you liked me too."

Elise jumped from the swing before they reached the

ground. She spun, wild shadows climbing the walls as she moved through the lantern's light. Catching the swing's ropes with both hands, she faced Julian, trapped him. "I do. I probably love you; I've been sweet on you my whole life."

"Then why . . . ?"

"I'm the only one," Elise said distantly. She swiped tears from her face, harder than she needed to. "My great-grandfather built our farm, Julian. The house, the barn, everything we have . . . it's been passed down to the firstborn, and sooner, not later, it's coming to me."

Struggling to understand, Julian stared. "What does that have to do with anything?"

Slowly, Elise backed away. "I can't be selfish and do as I please, Julian. I have to think about what comes next."

"I'd never ask you to give up your farm," Julian said.

"I know you wouldn't." She hesitated, and two more tears slipped down her face. Finally, resignation laced into the words, she said, "But I can't work it alone. And you can't do the kind of work it needs."

They both looked down. Disguised in a shoe mostly stuffed with leather, hiding beneath cotton pants, Julian's bad leg taunted. It hung too short; in the intermittent light, it seemed not only withered but gnarled.

At a distance, Julian heard Elise talking. Explaining that

fence lines needed to be walked and calving happened in fields, in the middle of the night.

He couldn't bear to look at her. Instead, he glanced at the wagon tucked in with the plow and the cutter. Charlie used to pull him to town in that wagon. These days, Julian used it in the fields, to push himself down rows of carrots and corn, beets and tomatoes — when they needed planting, or pinching back, or harvesting.

The world, the wide, limitless world, shrank to the size of the barn where he'd once lain fevering in the night. Gathering as much pride as he could, Julian swallowed his heart and said, "I hope nothing but the best for you."

Elise swayed, as if struck. When she spoke again, her voice came ragged and thin. "I wish you'd hate me."

"Well, I'm sorry, I don't." Standing, he didn't try to hide that he had to hop to get to his crutches. And he didn't bother to try to hide anything else, either. Picking up the lantern, he suffocated its flame. Deliberate, he hung it on a nail, and added, "I imagine Mama will cut you a piece of cake to take home."

He kept his back straight and his head high until he heard the door close behind her. The terrible stillness in his bones was building; a hard and ugly calm came over him. Then he dropped one crutch and tossed the other up to catch it by the foot. With perfect form, he twisted like a batter at home plate, and swung.

The lantern exploded. Hot glass and beads of kerosene marked him.

A few minutes later, Charlie popped his head inside. "Hey, Julie. You coming to your own party?"

"Yeah." Scrubbing his sleeve across his face, Julian retrieved his second crutch and went to leave. A fine spray of fire stung his brow; he couldn't tell if it was blood or blisters, but he didn't really care.

"Lord, baby brother. What did you do to your face?" Charlie asked. Then he caught a glimpse of the shattered lamp and put a hand out to stay him. Concerned, Charlie lowered his voice. "Hey now, what happened?"

Brushing his hand away, Julian pushed past him. He had a plan now: wash up, have some cake, and let this day die. But because Charlie liked to worry, and worse than that, liked to talk, Julian turned back.

"Nothing. It fell off the nail."

Charlie frowned. "Julian . . ."

"Nothing happened, Charlie. Are you coming or not?"

With another quick look at the wreckage, Charlie nodded. He was careful to shut the door firmly and to drop the pin in the latch.

Julian went back to his party and faked a hundred smiles. He ate cake, but skipped the ice cream, and opened his gifts slowly. There was a new watch from his parents and a chain from his brothers.

The sheet music from Elise, he burned later in private.

Six

As long as he moved from bench to bench through the night, Caleb found he could sleep in Central Park in downtown Los Angeles.

Bay trees hung low, crowded by sycamores and palms alike, darkening the paths in spite of the globe lights. The traffic on Olive Street never ceased, but then, the ocean had never been silent either. The constant hum of automobiles could seem like waves as long as Caleb closed his eyes.

Looking for work at The Pike had been a bad idea. A place like that let anybody hawk their wares; they didn't care if good people were abused or tormented or worse. Old rage ran in hot tributaries beneath his skin.

Unreeling himself, Caleb stretched his back and his knees, and both still hurt as he approached the marble fountain in the middle of the green. Today would be better; today, he'd stay in the city.

As he took off his hat, he stared into the uneven water, then dipped his hands into it. Splashing his face and neck, he hissed at the cold shock. It didn't clean like seawater. There was no scrub to it, no raw brace afterward when he lifted his face to the wind.

But this is what he had, and he would make do. He ignored the sideward glances thrown his way. He raised another handful and ran it through his hair. Let all of them in ironed shirts and new hats stare. They didn't work for a living, did they? Load of princesses, all of them, hands silky and perfumed.

When one hesitated, as if he might dare say something, Caleb made a rude gesture that sent him scurrying away. Who were they to say *anything* to him?

Dipping another handful of water, Caleb drank deep. He swished it around to chase the old, sour taste from his tongue. Right before he leaned over to spit it back in the fountain, a nearby police officer cleared his throat.

After The Pike, Caleb couldn't afford to draw more attention. He needed work; he needed a dollar to pay for a room, and a dinner that came hot on a plate instead of warm from the bins behind the Chinatown groceries.

Swallowing the water, Caleb put on a fake brogue and said, "Top of the morning to you."

The officer narrowed his eyes. "On your way to work, then, are you?"

Caleb didn't answer. Instead he wet his hand again and ran it through his hair as he stood. He knew he was being run off, but he couldn't be forced to do it quickly. He leveled his black eyes to meet the officer's gaze, a challenging cant to his shoulder.

In reply, the officer stroked his thumb down the gleaming club that hung at his hip.

Straightening his hat slowly with both hands, Caleb didn't even blink. He smoothed his vest, patted his trousers dry, then even took the time to retie both shoes.

"Daylight's burning," the officer said. His face dimmed in splotches, little crimson signs to confess his discontent, even if his voice stayed milky calm. "Don't want to be late, now, do you?"

"No, sir," Caleb said, his voice thick with sarcasm. "Be downright stupid to stand around wasting time for no reason. I'm not a stupid man."

No matter how fresh the morning air, no matter the spice

of bay that clung to the park and freshened each step through it, Caleb couldn't enjoy it. He was down to the clothes on his back, the shoes on his feet. Down to sleeping in parks and having nightmares about blood-wet calling cards.

Still annoyed, Caleb cut across the manicured lawn to the sidewalk. Cars jounced along beside him, the call of their horns like a flock of overexcited geese. They were stupid, graceless things, automobiles. Not like a ship on the waves, not graceful like those fine sailing girls at all.

Stepping in front of one, Caleb scraped his chin at the driver. Then he darted through a crowd of morning walkers to reach the shelter of a gold awning. The doors were locked, but Caleb waited until he saw motion inside and tapped on the glass.

"Not open," the man called through it. His disheveled tie and unbuttoned vest testified that he hadn't expected to see anyone so early.

Tapping again, Caleb pointed at the sign in the window. "Looking for work."

The man lit up and he hurried to unlock the door. His watery eyes skimmed Caleb's face, his damp shirt. But something made him smile anyway. "It's only service and maintenance right now, so you know."

Once, Caleb thought he might become a musician. Now

his hands were hard, trained for hauling fishing gear or lathing wood . . . or mopping floors and fixing chairs in Clune's Theatre Beautiful.

Offering his hand, Caleb said, "Fine by me."

"The office is right this way," the man said. "Having the hardest time getting this position filled, the war and all. Turned away any number of girls. Can you imagine?"

"Shame they don't know their place."

The man hummed agreeably, leading Caleb to a door at the end of a hall. Rounding his desk, he sorted through some papers until he found a half sheet and a pen. Glancing up from it, the man considered Caleb's clothes, his worn hat, once more before pressing on. "All right, then, I'll need your name for your packet . . ."

"Virgil," Caleb said, and leaned over to watch him write it. "V-i-r . . . That's right, and Walker."

If the manager suspected a lie, it never showed.

~~~~~~

The house was a lie. His life was a lie.

Julian stood in the front foyer, looking up the stairwell. Patterned carpet climbed one side of it, held down by brass tacks that Dad replaced every year on New Year's Day.

The other half was a scuffed flat built over the stairs — a

slide. Pressing fingers against his temple, Julian could summon a vague memory from before the slide. His pajamas had feet, and Sam's didn't; they always got sent to bed at the same time.

That was back when his bedroom was upstairs with the rest of his brothers'. After he came in from the barn, carried in because he couldn't walk, the pantry became his room. It wasn't noticeably pantrylike, except sometimes when the radiator came on, he smelled spiced apples. Somebody must have broken a jar of them in there before all the shelves came out and his desk and bed went in.

Sitting on the stairs, Julian hoisted himself up, step-by-step on his rear. The crutches rattled as he dragged them. At the top, he slid down polished floors, until he could get up and get his balance. Tucking his crutches under his arms, he slowly walked the hallway.

Cluttered with Tarzan novels and ripe with the scent of aftershave, Sam's room was exactly him. Mysteriously, a single roller skate dangled from a peg. Beside it hung a hosiery ad from a magazine — as close to a pin-up as Mama would allow in her house.

A messy spray of baseball cards teetered on the edge of the desk, a few drifting beneath Sam's bed. The quilt was made from patches of his old clothes, the ones that Julian couldn't wear, and old toys he'd grown out of. The velveteen in one square used to be a stuffed rabbit. A faded patch of gingham was once a pair of short pants.

Julian moved to the next room, the one with pale yellow wallpaper and curtains of white lace. Mama's black sewing machine sat in its clever cabinet, and an ironing board hung from the wall beside it. Shelves held dry goods, threads and buttons, bags of rags for future quilts. The air in there smelled like laundry brought off the line, and his mother's honey soap.

When he closed his eyes, Julian could see another version of this room. It was silver and blue, full of Charlie's things, with a full moon hanging in the window. The rasp of dried stalks coming for him sounded so real in his memories that Julian had to look out, to make sure.

A field of emerald green, the corn outside had begun to show its tassels. Bladed leaves cut through the wind, wavering and bent.

His heart seized, a trill caught below his collarbone. He wasn't afraid of the corn anymore, but the animal bit of his brain still took pause. Resting a hand on the frame, Julian breathed on the glass deliberately, then watched the fog fade. This was the last place he'd ever stood on two healthy legs, on two steady feet.

Somehow, they'd made him forget everything. That he watched the corn from Charlie's room and used to have a bed in Sam's. That there was a time when he walked up the stairs and back down, when he wasn't tucked in the pantry or carried anywhere. That they used to go to the church in Connersville, the one with impressive steps. Once, Julian was sure, he'd climbed a tree and gone ice-skating.

Polio had wiped it all away, and his family had helped disguise it.

There were hooks in the downstairs rooms for his crutches. His chores kept him in his mother's garden or tending the chickens; he detasseled corn and snapped beans. He put laundry on the lines and took it down again, but someone else hauled it inside.

Bitterness rose in Julian's throat. He was older than Dad had been when he went out West alone, and he had nothing. Not a girl, not a piece of land, nothing — wait, not true. He had a morbid, ugly gift that his parents warned him to hide. The one extraordinary thing of his own, and they'd tried to erase that, too.

Leaning over, Julian stared at a dead fly on the window sash. A surge of reckless discontent filled him; it blotted out reason and contemplation. Drawing a deep breath, Julian blew on the fly. Its iridescent wings trembled, then it staggered across the sash.

The flash of oblivion came on hard. It was a swift

punishment, and brief. Julian clutched the side of the window, his knee buckling beneath his weight. He blinked, and everything came back at once. All but sound; the ringing in his ears drowned that out.

Revived, Julian slid downstairs, almost crashing into the front door. Wrenching himself upright again, he threw open the door and stepped onto the porch. Blood still sang in his ears, his pulse thin and wild. With a single breath, he revived the captives in a spider's web, then clung to a rail for the aftermath. His heart quivered tentatively before catching its beat again.

As he stood there, he noticed a stiff, bent wing in the grass. He'd never tried to revive anything bigger than his pinkie. Somehow, that had seemed too great. Too godly. Cold crept over him.

It would have been easy to go back inside, to live in this oversized crib and blind himself to the truth once more. It would have been easy, and he'd never have been able to face himself again.

Hopping down the stairs, Julian nudged the bird with his crutch. Hardened in its pose, the bird — a sparrow — seemed insubstantial. It could have been made of papier-mâché. A light breeze ruffled the feathers, and Julian dropped down before he could think it through.

He burned all the breath from his lungs, but nothing happened. Still stiff, still dead, the sparrow lay on the grass, unmoving. With a sigh, Julian sat back. Nothing, just nothing. He should have known. Pressed by the sun, he reached for his crutches.

Abruptly, the sky changed angles. Beneath him, the earth shifted. Razored heat cut through him from the inside. He didn't feel it when he hit the ground. Streaks of green crossed his vision. A fine veil of panic drifted over him. Everything hurt; nothing moved. When he breathed, he gagged on the stench of decay.

The sparrow stirred. Its limbs moved contrary to nature: talons flexing against the joints, and its head wrenched nearly backwards. Its eyelids dragged over milky, sightless orbs. Lurching through the grass, it fell over, then righted itself. Claws spasmed, wings jerked.

Skin itching like pestilence, Julian wanted to move; he tried to crawl away. But he was frozen, eyes fixed open. Light burned, but tears wouldn't come. There was no blessed darkness for him. He had to see it, when the sparrow remembered how to flap its wings. The sight of maggots dropping from newly animated flesh branded him.

He prayed in formless desperation. All that mattered was ending this. He wanted it to stop, the bird, his own body, everything. Anything. The sparrow opened its beak and screamed. It was a high, ragged note, full of agony. Then the poor beast collapsed in silence.

"Thank you," Julian rasped. He almost sobbed when the violent grip on his body finally relaxed. Trembling, cold, he closed his eyes and basked in the dark, in taking a breath untainted by death.

Footsteps approached, and Henry leaned over, blocking out the sun. "What are you doing down there?"

Pushing up on his elbows, Julian shook his head a little too hard. Pain swirled through it, and his stomach turned in unison. "Nothing."

"Well, get up. Mama's going to have a conniption if she finds out you're playing with dead birds again."

"Again?" Julian asked.

But Henry hauled him to his feet and was gone before he got an answer. Still unsettled, Julian didn't follow. Instead, he pushed the sparrow's body into the bushes. After all that, it deserved to sink back into the earth in peace.

Julian went to wash up with the brown lye soap Mama kept in the laundry — when he was done, he decided, he'd find out what else they'd been keeping from him.

"Couldn't you leave him?" Mollie asked. She swept her hair behind her ear, offering her most winsome smile.

Sitting on the foot of Kate's bed, she'd already changed into her costume and dusted her skin with cornstarch to lighten it. A touch of rouge stained her lips; crushed charcoal darkened the lashes beneath her eyes. She was both beautiful and frightening, and she couldn't wait to get into the planter that would pose as a boat.

The smile, however, was lost on Kate. She hid beneath her quilt, changing the film in her camera. It wasn't particularly delicate work, but Handsome stood on her back while she did it, making the task more difficult. Mollie would shriek if he flapped his wings, and he would certainly flap his wings if Kate disturbed his balance, so like a surgeon, she made small, precise motions to balance everything.

"I think it should be romantic if we had a raven to circle your grave," Kate said.

Mollie narrowed her eyes at the bird. As far as she was concerned, he was a great, awful monster. She didn't care much for the fact that he fascinated Kate nearly as much as she did. Making a face, Mollie spoke, her voice far sweeter than her expression.

"It is *very* romantic," she said, rolling her eyes. "But he makes me nervous. I know it makes me a frightfully silly thing, but I won't be able to give my best performance. You said that film was dear."

Beneath the cover, Kate yelped when she closed her finger in the camera case. "It is, that's true . . ."

Slipping to her feet, Mollie backed toward the door. Any moment, Kate would stand up and that nasty bird would go wild. It was worse than a rat; rats had the sense to run away from human beings. "And I do so much want to impress Mr. Griffith with a perfect reel."

"Wouldn't that be something?" Kate's smile was evident in her voice, and she rose like a ghost. Uncovering one arm, she bobbed her shoulder to make Handsome work his way down. "He'd stare. Openly. In wonder! And I'd say, 'D.W., you're drawing flies, dear man. You must tell me exactly what you think.'"

Warming up to this fantasy, Mollie leaned her head against the door. "And he'd say, 'It's marvelous. It's wonderful. We'll want this for Triangle, straightaway.'"

"And I'll pretend to think about it. 'Oh, my, D.W., I don't know. Mabel Normand is doing such visionary work at Keystone right now . . .'"

"Don't be absurd," Mollie-as-D.W. roared.

Then she cried out, because Handsome spread his wings wide and roared back, "Nevermore!"

"Stop it," Kate said, shushing him as she shed the cover. "You're making my star nervous."

Pressing again, Mollie put on her most frail voice. "He really is, Kate. Please, let's leave him."

There was only so much daylight; they'd already missed the morning on account of a silvery blanket of fog. It was lovely to look at, but without the sea and the sky, and enough light to capture every flicker on Mollie's face, their film would be ruined. Mollie made certain she looked as nervous as she felt.

Kate relented. Opening the window, she nudged Handsome into flight. "Go to your home, darling. Go on. I'll treat you later with a bit of steak." Nudging again, she braced herself when he took off, both for the clutch of his claws and for Mollie's little scream.

"Better now?" Kate asked.

Lit with a dazzling smile, Mollie threw herself at Kate. Nearly tipping them over, she flung her arms around Kate's neck and hugged her expansively. Mollie's foil circlet fell off, and the silver charms on her wrists sang merrily. "*You're* marvelous! You're the best director in the world!"

"You can't say that yet," Kate mumbled, blushing.

"I can! I do!" Mollie kissed her cheek, then whirled away. Sweeping the circlet from the floor, she danced into the hallway, then turned back, beckoning. "Hurry, before we lose your precious light."

Kate grabbed her camera and satchel, and ran after her. It was brilliant, Mollie thought as they broke free across the sea grass and into the distance, that they got along so perfectly. With everything arranged, they'd be famous, *beyond* famous, hand in hand.

And if not hand in hand, then they'd each have someone to fondly remember from the balconies of their penthouse apartments, wouldn't they?

Seven

Draped in white paper, the kitchen resembled a hospital room. A terrible one, with a white-aproned madwoman presiding over a table full of cubed flesh. Zora used the back of her arm to brush hair from her face, then smiled when she saw Julian approaching.

"Perfect timing, baby sunflower. I need someone to crank for me."

His expression sullen, Julian moved to help with the grinder all the same. With a quick twist, he fastened the vise tight to the table. Once it was fixed in place, he turned the crank; it spun easily. Inside the grinder, metal teeth gnashed in anticipation.

Zora fed bits of pork and fat into the thing, matching her pace to Julian's. It was quiet, gory work, occasionally made exciting when Zora dipped her fingers a little too close to the workings of the grinder. She feared no machine on the farm and had the scars to prove it.

"You've been quiet today," Zora said.

Answering with a shrug, Julian turned the catching bowl so it wouldn't overfill on one side. He moved automatically, his hands trained in the art of making sausage. He knew when to tighten the vise, when to reverse the crank to retrieve a bit of bone before it ended up in the casings.

"Is something bothering you?"

Julian shook his head.

"You can talk to me," Zora said. She rounded the table, mostly to see if she could catch his eye from the other side. She couldn't, but she continued anyway. "About anything."

Mostly, she meant about Elise: She wanted to know why Elise had left the party early, what she'd said to put Julian in such a black mood. When he finally decided to answer, Zora expected a bit of romantic agony. What she got was something else entirely.

"Henry said I used to play with dead birds."

Slow to reply, Zora kept working. "They weren't dead long. I suppose you realize that."

"I don't remember anything."

Zora gathered herself, then sighed. "Your father and I

made you stop. The fits you have when you do it . . . they frightened us."

For no good reason, Julian bristled at her choice of words. "They're not fits. It gets dark, that's all."

"No. You die." She covered the mouth of the grinder with her hand and waited for him to stop cranking. Once he raised his head, she said, "With the bugs, it was nothing. A blink. The birds, a moment, and that was awful enough. Then I found you dead in the yard, guarded by a dog we'd buried that morning."

Outwardly, Zora was steady. She was always steady: broken bones and accidents in the field, a fire in the feed house, the creek flooding the back forty — steady. Whatever the disaster, she stared at it, decided how to conquer it, and briskly went about the business of doing so.

She told this particular story the same way. It was over and done with now. At the time, she'd clutched Julian to her chest and, with bared teeth, dared anyone to take his body from her. The half-moon bruises she'd left on his arms took weeks to fade.

"You woke up when the funeral director knocked on the door. And after that, we kept you very close. Kept the yard clean as we could, and yes, we hoped you'd forget entirely."

Julian cranked again when Zora nudged him. "I didn't."

"We still had to try to protect you from yourself."

There was a darkness to his quiet, something beyond contemplation. His shoulders hardened. Still, he kept his voice low, as if he were ashamed to talk back to her. "You're only afraid because you don't understand."

"Oh, do you think?"

Stubborn, Julian muttered, "I know."

Picking up a measured cup of water, Zora said, "Look at me." When he did, Zora threw the water into the air.

Before Julian could dodge, the water exploded into thousands of individual beads. They swirled around him, crystalline and catching the light from outside. Hands folded, Zora admired the rainbows that flickered across Julian's dumbstruck face.

Water came so much more easily these days. Sometimes at night, she dreamt of slipping into it. She liked it when Emerson sat by the aluminum tub, because every so often, she thought if she were left alone in the water, she might melt into it. Disappear into it.

Only once, last winter, she admitted that. And in reply, Emerson said, "There's times when I think the earth wants me back." Zora remembered it as clearly as she did Julian's half-moon bruises, as clearly as the silver streams running beneath the prairies.

Silent, she turned her head ever so slightly, and the water exploded again. Beads became mist, a swirl of fog that hung improbably over the table.

Meeting her son's eyes, Zora raised her brows and watched him. The fog swirled. Like a raincloud, it grew denser. Then, abruptly, it spun, a hurricane summoned, a delicate typhoon.

Glittering flecks of water clung to their hair like a liquid veil. The kitchen cooled; it tasted clean, like an afternoon after rain. Zora again raised the measuring cup, and the storm drained into it.

"I understand so much more than you can imagine, Julian Thomas."

Wonderstruck, Julian stared at the measure as his mother put it on the table. It was half-full now, the rest of its contents still misting his skin, his hair. Unsteady in spite of his crutches, he found it took more than a moment to compose his thoughts.

"I got it from you? Why didn't you tell me?" Scrubbing his face dry with his sleeve, he bobbled. "What else are you keeping from me?"

Weary, Zora brushed him aside to work the grinder herself. She still tasted the water in the air; it called from the pump and the spring and the stream. It called from everywhere, whispering sweetly, trying to entrance. Focusing on the work in front of her, Zora fed the grinder with one hand and cranked with the other.

"Nature demands a balance. It won't let you disturb the proper course of the world."

Now frustrated, Julian asked, "What does that mean?"

"You don't create life, duck." Zora leveled her cool blue gaze at him. "You *trade* it."

And then, while Julian's mouth still hung agape, Zora went back to making sausages. Dinner couldn't wait for dramatics or confessions. Once he recovered, she told him about the water that flowed through her and the earth that bound his father.

It was his birthright. No matter how fervent their prayers otherwise, it wasn't going away.

~~~~~

The set was perfect. The restless sea clawed at a darkening sky, and Mollie was a gem on a greens-laced planter. It was made of concrete, big enough to water a horse in — or to bury the Lady of Shalott. Heaps of fragrant lilac made her bed, set off by handfuls of creamy honeysuckle.

The costume was the same: a long white gown made more

interesting with bits of gold foil and beads. They'd brushed Mollie's hair until it gleamed like liquid sunset, and let it pour over the sides of the makeshift boat.

Kate bit her own lips to keep from crying. She advanced the film steadily, turning the camera on its tripod to take in the entirety of the scene. But grief poisoned her; it cracked her open and left her wounded.

Her father was right. He was awful and horrible and right. When she was done, all she'd have would be a shadow play: ghosts caught pretending at life.

Without color, without the palette of gilt ornaments and gold hair, skin pale as death, and the endlessly grieving sea, no one would see the truth. Regal and still, a spray of flowers clutched beneath her chin, Mollie had truly *become* the Lady of Shalott. She had died for want of Lancelot before Kate's stunned eyes, and no one would ever know.

"How is it?" Mollie asked, her lips barely moving.

"Terrible." Kate swallowed her sobs, but the tears freely marked her cheeks. "You can get up. We're done."

Mollie combed fingers through her hair. "What's the matter? Didn't you get what you wanted?"

"It's not you," Kate said, camera cradled in her lap as she unscrewed it from the tripod. Miserable, she tried to ignore the stone in her chest, growing and growing by the moment.

Mollie lifted her hems and came to sit beside Kate. "Did I move and ruin it? I thought I felt a spider on my cheek, but I did try to stay still."

Mournfully, Kate lurched to the side and dropped her head onto Mollie's shoulder. "No, you were wonderful. It's me. I want something that's impossible. Nothing ever looks so amazing on my reels as it does in my head. It's like . . . I don't know what it's like."

"Knowing there's cake and you can't have any?" Mollie smiled crookedly. "That always makes me cross."

"No, it's more than that. Or less than that. It sounds ridiculous, trying to explain it. But I've got so many feelings inside me: I imagine such glorious things. But I can't make them real." Trying valiantly for a careless smile, Kate shrugged. "It's no one's fault I'm ordinary."

Mollie gasped. Hopping to her feet, she grabbed Kate's hand and dragged her to standing. "If I thought you'd stay there, I'd make you stand in a corner!"

"I — " Kate said, but Mollie cut her off.

"No! I'm going to wash your mouth out with soap." Mollie balanced the tripod on her shoulder and pointed toward the house imperiously. "Right this instant. March."

Slipping her camera into its satchel, Kate laughed faintly. "You're mad."

"Then we're all mad here." Mollie poked at her. "How can you say you're ordinary? You're remarkable! Maddeningly unique!"

"You haven't seen any of my developed film yet," Kate protested.

"I don't mean that." Mollie waved a hand, ignoring Kate's fallen expression. "That 'something' you can do, Kate. You can stop time, and you think you're ordinary?"

With a sigh, Kate turned toward home. "You can't do anything with thirty seconds. It's entirely useless. I know people who can . . ."

Mollie's eyes grew round as she waited for Kate to finish.

The familiar strings of secrecy tightened round Kate's throat. Her gifts, her parents', were no secret at home. True enough, Mimi never sat sunsets anymore. There was too much pain in seeing the future, she said. What little pleasure she could find in her clairvoyance was never enough to risk its torments.

But Daddy was forever whisking them away on the wind. It was a useful gift, and his best plaything, too. He'd carried Kate to the tops of the pyramids and into the boughs of the tallest trees. It was impossible to win a game of catch with him, for he could blink away at any moment.

What's more, in all the years they'd traveled, meeting artist friends at the fairs, flinging themselves to the far corners of every known map, Kate had met hundreds of people gifted by the elements.

There was a French woman in Virginia who could make the wind speak with any voice she chose. She would have gotten on brilliantly with the old grandfather in Prussia — he could make fire's embers carry messages for him across the miles.

Two black-eyed twins in Cyprus witched water together: the girl leaned toward heat and steam, the boy toward cold and ice. They taught Kate to ice-skate on a white-sand beach and to kiss beneath an olive tree, which made for a lovely summer indeed.

But it was a private society. Kept quiet, discussed only among those touched by it. And even to them, Kate was an oddity. She'd been explained away as aether, a fifth element made from the other four.

Heaven, or space, or air to breathe: aether simply *was*. Like her gift — it *existed*. Stopping time for thirty seconds at a time was good for nothing but sneaking out of the house or catching a dropped cup before it shattered on the floor.

"Who can what?" Mollie prompted.

" . . . Bend their arms and fingers the wrong way," Kate finally said. "Pound spikes into their eyes and survive. And eat fire! You really haven't lived until you've spent the night with fair people. The ones *in* the attractions, not the ones attending. You'll never know nicer folk than the Wolf People of the Sierra Madre."

Whirling round, Mollie nearly took Kate's head off with the tripod. "You're making that up."

"I'm not, and I can prove it. I've got films. You'll see. Come on."

Clutching her satchel with both arms, Kate broke into a run up the path. Her mood soared like mercury in glass — there was a reason she wanted to paint with light and motion. She didn't need color! Or scent, or sensation! Sometimes it was enough to *see*. With her camera she could prove impossible things, record beautiful things, create perfect things. She could slip past disbelief and into truth.

Suddenly giddy, Kate wanted to leap and spin. She settled for scrambling across the grass with Mollie at her heels.

But she stopped short when she saw a man with a handcart taking away an armoire.

"Oh no," Kate murmured, and hurried for the back door.

In a single afternoon, her parents had transformed the house. Sheets covered the furniture and mirrors; they belonged to the house, not the Witherspoons. The movers were taking away the extras they'd hired, like the armoire and the blue velvet chair Daddy liked to nap in, even the whimsical place settings embossed with images of the sun.

Amelia turned when Kate stepped inside, her awareness unerring. "Did you finish your movie, sweetheart?"

Ignoring her question, Kate peeled off her satchel. "You said we weren't going yet."

"We'll have one last night here. Mollie can celebrate with us."

"She's got nowhere to go!"

"She does," Amelia smiled brightly. "Your father and I had breakfast with Mrs. Collins. You know her. She owns the theatre by the boardwalk. She said if Mollie needed a place to stay, there are apartments above the stage, and of course plays that need actresses all the time."

Trembling with rage, Kate wanted so badly to throw things. To break things. She wanted to kick holes in the floor and throw rocks through the window until her mother's awful smile shattered along with the glass.

But instead, she ground her teeth together and forced a smile when she looked to Mollie. "How exciting. You'll be an independent woman of means, Mollie."

Pale eyes darting between Amelia and Kate, Mollie found a smile and played along. "An apartment of my very own!"

"Please don't be offended," Amelia told Mollie, taking her by the elbow, "but Kate's father and I took the liberty of paying the first month's rent. We couldn't stand the idea of Kate's dearest friend sleeping on the beach."

It was lies, Kate thought. The smile stung to hold; she positively ached, trying to pretend this was lovely and wonderful and not an absolutely deliberate attempt to separate the two of them. "I'll send you reams of letters, Mollie."

Amelia smoothed her hair back with fluttering hands. "Why don't the two of you freshen up for dinner? We're dining downtown tonight. Won't that be fun?"

"Oh yes," Kate said, already backing toward her bedroom. "Ever so much." Then, as soon as she and Mollie were closed up tight behind her bedroom door, Kate dropped her false front and said, "I'm not going."

Mollie frowned. "To dinner?"

"No. *Away.*"

Whirling around the room, Kate plucked a music box from her dresser. A few warbled notes played when she turned it over. Manipulating the base, she revealed a hidden drawer.

Kate produced a roll of bills tied with ribbon. She'd been saving for ages, waiting for exactly the right time. Holding it up for Mollie's inspection, Kate smiled again. But now it was genuine.

"I think they're waiting for us in Hollywood, don't you?"

It was easy to get lost in Clune's, Caleb discovered.

Behind the canvas screen was a labyrinth of halls and cubbies, as well as iron stairs that swirled into the old catwalk. A cache of crosses and altars stayed polished, but locked in a room used only for storage.

Old green rooms and costume rooms and sitting rooms filled the attic space. No one dressed or painted themselves there now. The stage plays and church services had been replaced by a projector and a single bright light.

The auditorium stretched back a hundred yards at least, the balcony nearly as long. Gold-decked boxes hung on either side of the movie palace. A dome rose above the seats, its spokes banding toward an ornate cap.

Standing on a scaffold to replace burned-out bulbs, Caleb told one of the other fellas from maintenance that it reminded him of St. Peter's Basilica.

"You're something rare, ain't ya?" the man said, laughing as he went back to his paints and brushes.

The question left Caleb cross. There wasn't anything rare about knowing that. Anyone, idiot or genius, could go inside the basilica, as long as he felt like standing in line for his turn. Butcher or barber, deckhand or priest, they let anybody have a look if they wanted one.

When Caleb caught the first passing ship out of Baltimore, he ended up in Liverpool. For a while, he worked the shipyards, then figured out he could go farther if he worked the ships.

As a tender, he shoveled coal and grew pale as a cave fish — not that anyone knew. Black dust peppered his hands; it slipped into the weave of all his shirts. He worked his way up from the bowels and the boilers, into maintenance, and eventually crew.

But always on freight ships. The liners that raced the Atlantic carried *people*, East Coasters, newspaper readers. And it was a long time ago, what happened in Baltimore, but people had good memories for murder.

So he went on ships full of bananas and books, stuffed with crates of unnamable goods and bottles of irreplaceable wine. And those ships went everywhere; he'd seen the world. He'd stood in St. Peter's Basilica and stared into its dome. It was all heaven up there in blue and gold, angels and saints gazing back down.

That's what it was like on a ship, on deck. Nothing but water below and heaven above. Hard work eased the constant tension in his blood. Hammering ice off a deck was good, clean distraction. Hauling ropes burned his aggression down to an ember that needed no tending.

Come shore leave, he could always find a boxing ring that would take him, 'til the next ship set out for Persia or

Anatolia. He'd still be on the water if not for the war. He was already hunted for somebody else's crimes. He wasn't about to go down with another Lusitania; like hell would he die for somebody else's scrap.

If things were *right* in the world, if there was *justice* in it, he'd have been at home in Baltimore with his wife. With his life, the one he was supposed to have. The one he was promised. The one *she* stole from him.

Shooting Thomas Rea was an accident. Burning the rowhouse, that was incidental.

Too bad Caleb was the only one who saw it that way.

Eight

Amelia woke with a start, bursting out of dreams of fire to stare into the dark.

She'd had that dream too often of late, of the sun growing until it consumed her. It stretched brilliant arms across the sunset, gathering her in tendril fingers. Instead of reducing her to ash, she became part of the flame; she twisted with it, disappeared into it. It wasn't a nightmare. That's what made it terrible.

But that's not what woke her.

Fire still danced on her skin, heat that dissipated when she threw the covers back. Something was wrong. Missing, but she couldn't place it. Though the house was shuttered, closed to wait for the next tenants, it was too quiet.

Slipping from bed, she found the floor cold under her feet. That chased away the last of her heat. Wrapped in one of Nathaniel's old shirts, she pulled on her robe and took her time with the tie.

The walls seemed to stretch too high. The moonlight through the windows shone too bright. Unnerved by the quiet, she rounded the bed and stood at Nathaniel's feet.

With his face buried in the pillows, Nathaniel was nothing but a dark figure in the sheets, one that smelled faintly of musk and bay rum.

Slipping her fingers under the covers, Amelia trailed across the rough curve of his heel, up the shapely curve of his calf. Every inch of him was as familiar as her own body; she scored him gently with her nails.

He shifted beneath her touch. Still sleeping, he reached for her, hand skimming through the emptiness she'd left in the bed. At once, he sat up. His mussed hair fell in a wave across his eyes; his expression soft and smeared from sleep. Lips still, he spoke to her all the same.

What's the matter?

Unexpected relief flooded through Amelia. Like some part of her had doubted their connection for that moment. Squeezing his ankle, she said, *Something's amiss.*

Nathaniel scrubbed a hand through his hair and looked

around. There was nothing boyish about him now. Hard angles informed his jaw, and a refined edge smoothed his brow. Only his eyes were the same, narrow and dark; his mouth still lush when he pursed it, concentrating.

I don't hear anything, he told her.

At once, Amelia stiffened. It wasn't the quiet. It was the stillness. The rhythm was gone. It began the day Kate was born, a constant thrum that marked their days together, fading only when they were apart. When their family was complete, it had a pulse of its own — and that's what had stopped.

Realizing it at the same moment, Nathaniel threw off the covers. Together, they hurried down the hall. White sheets fluttered as they passed, ghosts of furniture now forgotten.

Footsteps whispered in the dark, echoing through the nearly empty house. Reaching Kate's door, Amelia didn't bother to knock. She already knew, but needed the proof.

The bed was empty.

Reaching back, she clutched Nathaniel's arm. *See if Handsome's still here.*

Nathaniel kissed her hand when he peeled it from his arm, then disappeared down the hall. Long stripes of moonlight cut the path in jagged edges. While he looked outside,

Amelia searched the remains of Kate's room. The camera, gone. The tripod, left behind —

A hot, fresh wound split her when she pulled the covers back. Kate's little pillow, the velvet one Zora had sewn to welcome her to the world, was gone. Though it was threadbare, worn smooth from little hands, it was still precious. The one thing that always meant Kate was at home.

At the same moment, Nathaniel murmured into her, *Handsome's not in his cage.* Sinking to her knees, Amelia pressed her face against the mattress and started to cry.

They'd raised a creature insubstantial and untamable, a daughter of fire and wind. Their beloved girl, from nowhere and everywhere, was gone.

～～～

Deep in thought, Julian set the table for dinner by reflex alone. The kitchen was more crowded than usual, with Zora turning fried chicken while Charlie's fiancée, Marjorie, whipped parsnips by the basin. Charlie himself minded the biscuits, not that they really needed minding. It kept him close to his girl.

They all may as well have been in the next county. Julian rubbed spots from forks, his thoughts churning and repeating. His mother had a secret, she had a gift. Had it come on her the same way his had, in the throes of disease?

A haze softened most of his memories of being sick, the edges faded pale and indistinct. But he knew — from memory or from the telling of it — that she'd come down with polio too. Not near as bad — she could walk, but the disease had sapped some of the strength from her hands.

That's why he did most of her churning, her cranking — he was the one who ran the laundry through the wringer, the one who ground the family's coffee in the little black mill.

Was it a trading? His legs, her hands, for their gifts? An accounting by God, to pay for the loss? Except that didn't make sense. He couldn't feature a celestial ledger that tallied disadvantages and paid out magic.

By that logic, Helen Keller should have been able to transform wheat sheaves into gold while gliding above them in sorcerous flight.

Less fantastically, it didn't explain his father's gift, though Julian had to admit: he hadn't seen Emerson change the earth. Part of him discounted it completely.

"Is that Sam?" Marjorie asked. She leaned toward the window, uncertain laughter lacing her words. "Goodness, what's he done to his hair?"

Julian turned as Sam came through the door. He hadn't

just cut his shaggy hair. Gone were his dungarees, replaced by the olive drab cotton of a doughboy uniform. His hobnailed boots clicked on the bare floor. Throwing his arms out, he turned to let everybody get a look at his taped-up britches and the tight fit of the jacket across his shoulders. "What do you think?"

"Real funny," Charlie said.

Zora paled and put her tongs aside. The chicken hissed on in the hot grease, imitating the sound of rain in the distance. "I never thought I'd say this, but I certainly hope you're mocking your brother, young man."

"No, ma'am," Henry said, coming in the door behind Sam. He wore the same uniform, had the same haircut. It didn't suit him at all.

Julian watched his mother wind herself tight. New steel slipped into her spine, and she drew her shoulders back as if she might march off to the Western Front herself. Instead, she marched up to Sam and Henry, oblivious to the fact that they towered over her.

"Have you both lost your minds?" she demanded.

"It was coming anyway," Henry said. Shifting uncomfortably, he tugged the hem of his jacket. "Once they called Charlie, it was just a matter of waiting 'til it was us."

"Anyhow, Papa said it's all over except for the crying," Sam insisted.

"If that were true, they wouldn't need the draft, now would they?" she snapped.

"This way, we get to pick our specialty. They don't shoot the signal corps, Mama."

"It's a war, Samuel. They shoot *everyone!*"

The Birch farm had always been a peaceful place; the boys got loud, but the parents had never needed to raise their voices.

Henry looked to Charlie for help. But if he thought Charlie would defend them, he was schooled otherwise.

Crossing his arms, Charlie nodded toward the fields out back, to the farm. "Bad enough I have to go. Who's going to bring in the corn this year? Who's going to mow the hay? Julie sure can't."

The words stung Julian. A little at first, but the ache spread like blood on tissue. The rest of the conversation turned to noise in his ears. As he slipped from the kitchen, he heard them going on about sending pay packets home to hire farm hands, and how Sam wasn't even old enough to be conscripted yet.

Julian came back to the table for dinner, but it was an ugly meal, full of make-believe. Everyone used their best manners and flattest voices. The food tasted like ash, and no one laughed, not once. Not a single time.

Julian couldn't look at any of them. He'd failed his

parents by default, lost Elise before he even had her, and couldn't measure himself by his brothers anymore. The truth was, they'd suspended him in a perfect bubble. Acted like he was the same as them, but secretly believed he never would be.

So that night, he stayed inside while his parents and brothers argued over coffee on the back porch. Something about the night air, or maybe darkness, made it easier for them to yell themselves hoarse. It also made it easier for Julian to steal the two hundred dollars his mother kept in a coffee can above the stove.

Shutting up his bedroom, he left by the front door. It was morning before anyone realized he was gone, and by then, he was on a train bound for Chicago. From there, he'd head west. The scent of honeysuckle and the memory of the siren, the girl he'd always seen against an ocean sunset, beckoned.

She was as good a compass as any.

For most of the passengers onboard, the train's gentle sway was a lullaby. Men in smart uniforms had come through hours ago to douse the lights in the car, leaving Kate to sit awake in the dark.

She couldn't even lean her head against the window.

Mollie had claimed that seat and now dozed against a back-drop of scrub-dotted mountains. Even Handsome slept. His talons cut into the back of Kate's seat. Every so often, he'd shuffle his wings, a dark harbinger over her shoulder.

Kate wrapped her arms around her pillow and sighed. If she could see the ocean, things would be so much better. The first time she'd stepped foot in San Diego, she felt a familiar caress on her skin — the same touch she always felt when she held off time.

There was the smallest part of her afraid that she was heading in the wrong direction. What if this was the last summer she'd see him? What if they were meant to meet? What if she should have stayed in San Diego or boarded a southbound train for Mexico?

The questions spun round and round in her head. Staring at the ceiling only made her think. Thinking made her worry. Worrying made her doubt. It grew like a knot in her belly, filling her with a terrible, unraveled skein.

It could take weeks to get her film back from the devel-oper. Without *The Lady of Shalott* to show the studios, she had nothing. They'd have to make do in the meantime, but Kate had no idea how far her little bank roll would go. What did it cost to let a room? How much would they pay for two breakfasts and dinners a day?

Mollie could get work straightaway at a dancehall or a

movie palace — they loved having pretty girls up front to lure customers. Whether Kate was pretty enough for those jobs, she didn't know. But since she only had the clothes on her back, and those clothes were her father's, she thought it unlikely she'd be hired to dance for dimes.

The knot grew a bit more, because she realized she had no idea what boys — what anyone, really — did for a living. She'd never had a permanent home, never attended classes in a schoolhouse. Her world was made of nomads and artists, expatriates and wanderers.

Daddy sold paintings sometimes. He and Mimi hired themselves out to create art for the World's Fairs. They never had to pay train fare. Only rarely did they rent a house — there were friends enough the world over to keep them through their travels.

Until that very moment, in the hushed warmth of the train, Kate had never considered whether her family was poor or wealthy, or how they got by. They simply did, and now she suspected it was by a magic she didn't possess.

An uneven beat flickered through her heart, and she folded herself more tightly into the seat. The flicker raced through her again, and Kate couldn't catch her breath. There was a weight pressing on her, and it threatened to flatten her completely. Reaching across the armrest, she nudged Mollie.

"Are you awake?" she asked, knowing she wasn't. Kate shook her again, shushing Handsome when he stretched his wings wide above them.

Mollie wriggled a bit and mumbled, "What?"

Leaning closer, Kate whispered to keep from waking the other passengers. "What sort of work do you think might suit me?"

"You're a director, goose."

"No, I mean until then." The armrest dug into Kate's ribs, and she nudged Mollie again. "It's not a joke; we've got to get by until our reel is finished."

That made Mollie lift her head. "I thought we finished it this morning."

"The photography, yes." Kate curled over the armrest, wishing very much she could lay her head on Mollie's shoulder. "I've got to send it to Eastman to develop. It won't take long, but . . . oh no."

Wary, Mollie sat up. "What?"

"They have to send it back. What address am I going to give them?"

Cutting Handsome a dark look, Mollie stretched herself in her seat until she was smoothed out and entirely awake. Though she didn't seem worried, she was as serious as Kate had ever seen her. She asked, "How much do you have?"

"A bit more than a hundred dollars. And it'll cost fifteen dollars to have the reel developed, so figure that in."

Mollie scribbled in her palm with her fingernail. "A furnished flat is expensive. A boarding house is much better. Cheaper, and they feed you sometimes. Some of them do. We'll say you're my brother, so they won't argue about renting to us. You look young enough."

An unnerved shiver ran up Kate's spine. She hadn't even considered that. There was so much to know, so many things to plan for, and it was suddenly, overwhelmingly obvious that she had not the first clue where to start.

Fortunately, it seemed Mollie did. "We should buy a paper, first thing. There will be ads in the back. We'll go through them all if we have to. It shouldn't take long."

Some of the knot loosened. "What about jobs?"

"There's all sorts." Mollie closed her hand and smiled. "If there's a boardwalk, we should try there first. Even if it's sweeping up or selling popcorn, it'll be more fun than a typing pool."

"You're so clever," Kate said, her admiration spilling out in three little words. But it was all true. Mollie knew everything important. She was an extraordinary actress too.

It couldn't have been sheer luck that they met when they

did. Kate had been going to Palais de Danse since the fair opened its doors; hundreds of times at least!

It had to be fate that she'd found Mollie there on her very last visit. Or destiny, or providence . . . something more than happenstance, anyway. Muses didn't sprout from fig trees; they didn't fall from the sky.

Catching Mollie's hand, Kate squeezed it and swore, "This *will* be wonderful."

Squeezing back, Mollie relaxed against the window again. "I'm going back to sleep. Unless you've got another crisis brewing?"

"I don't, I swear," Kate said. But she didn't let go.

It was a long way to Los Angeles, and she needed her lucky charm.

Nine

Emerson stood at the back door, considering his boys.

They wandered the yard in their uniforms, talking low and casting furtive looks at the house. The preacher was coming, and Marjorie's parents, too. There were roses in the boys' buttonholes, and a white-flour cake was cooling in the window.

The wedding was never going to be grand, rushed as it was. But it should have been merrier. Emerson whipped the bowl of buttercream as Zora tried to brighten the kitchen. She unfurled her nicest tablecloth and stared into the distance while she did it.

Sometimes, her gaze would stray toward Emerson, revealing the raw, wounded animal she'd trapped inside her apron and best Sunday dress.

Julian had been missing for a week. No letter, no telegram . . . the only relief so far was no word of a body found in a creek or runoff ditch. They couldn't stop their lives for him. The army wasn't about to wait for its new doughboys. The fields needed water; the chickens wanted feed.

"Dad," Charlie said, starting up the porch steps. "We've been talking, and we don't want you to worry about the farm. We're going to send home as much as we can."

Leaning against the counter, Emerson shook his head. "We'll mind the farm."

"You can't do it alone." Charlie brushed his fingers against the screen, instead of opening the door. It was like confession when he said, "I didn't know they were going to do this."

"Didn't think you did," Emerson reassured him.

Pressing a hand against the door frame, Charlie closed his eyes, then finally said, "Marjorie and I can go to the city-county building. She's going to want a real wedding afterward anyway, and it doesn't seem right . . ."

Zora straightened the tablecloth. "You're not taking back your wedding day, Charlie. Let's try to enjoy it."

"Mama . . ."

Warning, Zora said, "Charlie."

"Mind your mother," Emerson said.

His being the oldest showed, in the way he hesitated, and the way he made himself walk away instead of arguing. They could tell him not to think about it, but he would. He had two well-meaning idiots for brothers, going off to Europe with him . . . and he was missing one stupid spoiled brat who should have stayed home.

Julian had always been his, sort of. Being seven years older, Charlie felt like an extra father. He taught Julian to walk twice, once when he was a fat baby with a rooster comb of thin gold hair. And again when he was a skinny, wobbly boy down to one leg and a pair of crutches.

Maybe he should have pushed more about what happened in the barn on Julian's birthday. Or he should have heard him leaving the house. How far could he get on his own? Charlie'd driven to Indianapolis looking for him; Henry and Sam got as far as Zionsville before coming back without him.

Reading Charlie's face, Emerson gently kicked the door to get his attention. "I said mind your mother, Charlie. It is what it is."

Charlie dragged a hand down his face. "Yes, sir."

"It is what it is," Zora repeated once Charlie had rejoined his brothers in the yard.

Carrying the buttercream to the counter, Emerson

reached for the cake. His hands, so rough from working the land, were gentle when it came to frosting. Long fingers turned in elegant shapes, and he spoke deliberately.

"They're all grown, Zo. It was going to break our hearts no matter how they proved it."

"I'm glad you can be philosophical," she said.

"It's not philosophy, it's a fact. We can cry later when it's the two of us."

Taking up her scissors again, Zora attacked the bundle of daisies in the basin waiting to be trimmed and tied with ribbon. Flatly, she said, "I've already cried."

Emerson put his spatula aside. With careful scoops, he spooned icing into a cone of paper. His lips barely moved when he replied.

"Well, I haven't, so get ready."

~~~~~

Los Angeles wasn't quite what Kate expected.

They'd found a room to share at The Ems right away; it wasn't very expensive on account of the constant waft of garlic from a restaurant around the way. And jobs came quickly too, because Mollie knew where to ask.

The golden glow of the Los Angeles in Kate's mind and imagination faded after a few days. As she hurried from work to fetch Mollie, Kate couldn't help but notice all the things that made it a new city instead of an old fortress.

Orange and lemon groves surrounded the borders, and a bustling amusement park glittered on its shores.

But the city itself was a jumble of poured concrete and Spanish Mission architecture. Hand-painted advertisements abounded, competing with signs on top of signs on top of scaffolds bearing lighted signs.

The constant glow, exhilarating at first, devoured the nights, and automobiles roared away the silence. It was a city by the sea, but the only waves Kate noticed were tides of people, filling sidewalks and crossing streets. Each time the red streetcar passed, it shuddered to a stop and people gushed out in all directions.

To herself — only to herself — Kate admitted she was a bit disappointed. She'd grown up in well-worn lands, places that still stood but once had borne other names. *Londinium, Lutetia Parisiorum, Athēnai.*

She'd slept in ancient towers, bought pomegranates in bazaars that used to sell them to pharaohs and emperors and queens. Those cities bore new lights with dignity. Their narrow streets encouraged walking; they were paths first for human beings.

Los Angeles seemed made for *things*. It flourished on a grand scale, and so much of it was mechanical. Wires crossed overhead. Iron fire escapes climbed the buildings instead of ivy. Pavement yielded to glass, making way for machines instead of man.

Cramming her hat down a little tighter, Kate hurried through The Pike to find Mollie. Jostled and elbowed, she'd learned to push back.

Train conductors thought nothing of shoving her through doors, men thought nothing of stepping in front of her. Absolutely no one cared that she was *Amelia and Nathaniel's daughter*. She wasn't a pretty bit of porcelain anymore, and that was wonderful.

It was valuable, too, learning to move with authority, speaking up when she needed to be heard. It was, she decided, training her to be a proper director. Though Mollie was biddable enough, another actor might not be. Certainly, she couldn't ask a producer's *permission* to make films.

Weaving between concession wagons, Kate slowed when she finally caught sight of Mollie.

A scarlet confection, Mollie wore red from the plume in her hat to the points of her shoes. She'd even stained her lips to match, which made her teeth gleam like pearls when she threw her head back and laughed.

Two sailors flanked her, smart in their blue uniforms and white scarves. They were supposed to be interested in the iced soda she was selling. But the taller one kept fingering one of her loose curls, while the shorter one stared at her pretty mouth.

Something sharp pierced Kate's chest. Sweaty, and smelling faintly of spoiled ice cream and sick from the roller coasters, she cut through the crowd deliberately. Her workday emptying rubbish bins was over. Mollie should have been handing off her soda box to the next shift too.

"Hey, fellas," Kate said, too loud to be friendly. "My sister's something, isn't she?"

Both sailors took a step back, and the taller one laced his hands together. "Hey there, pal. Where'd you come from?"

The smile, Kate could tell, was thin and performed, and he spoke to her like she was both a baby and an idiot. The syrup flowed so thickly through his words, she could wade through it. Annoyed, Kate went to tell him exactly where she came from, but Mollie interrupted.

"He works the clean-up crew. Isn't that adorable?" Mollie laughed and leaned toward the sailor. A strange shadow ran through her expression, tense and specific. It wasn't for the sailors; it was for Kate.

Uneasy, Kate rubbed the back of her neck. "We'll miss the next car if we don't get going."

The shorter sailor dug a dime from his pocket. "Why don't you get yourself an Italian ice, kid? We'll make sure your sister gets home all right."

There was nothing menacing about them. Smooth faced and neatly pressed, they were just sailors — like the other servicemen who wandered The Pike before shipping off. Young and bright, with a little bit of money to spend and a long journey ahead. Still, Kate hesitated. "We always walk home together."

"What are you, twelve? Thirteen?"

Crossing her arms, Kate frowned. She didn't look *that* young. "Sixteen."

The taller sailor leaned over, pretending to confide. "Oh, even better. When I was your age, I was sneaking into the dancehalls. Ladies are starving for a dance with a gent, kid. Go on, live a little."

Mollie nodded, and beneath the icebox, she flicked her fingers, as if to shoo Kate away. "You'll be fine on your own, and so will I. *Really.* I'll see you tonight, for dinner."

"Maybe a little after dinner," the shorter sailor joked.

Trembling inside, Kate stood there a moment. Of course they treated her like a tagalong kid brother; she looked like one. But she wasn't about to be dismissed so easily. Shoving her hand out, she looked from Mollie to the sailors and said, "I hope I don't accidentally tell our Ma about this."

Mollie drew herself up, her face the same shade of crimson as the plume that brushed her cheek. The sailors, though, burst out laughing, and one dropped a quarter into Kate's palm. As she closed her fingers around it, he gave her a little shove to send her on her way.

With one last look over her shoulder, Kate saw that Mollie'd already turned away. Hurrying down the board-walk, Kate didn't raise her head. Thirty-five cents; they'd paid her a quarter and a dime to go away.

Enough for a movie palace matinee. A half-dozen bottles of Coca-Cola. A dinner plate and a piece of pie at Harvey House. Thirty-five cents.

She planned to repeat that over and over until Mollie got home. Now that Kate'd learned what things cost, she could count the things that money would buy.

It could be a prayer or a spell. A bit of ordinary magic, Kate hoped as she stumbled through the crowd. Maybe that would loosen the unforgiving knot inside her.

~~~~~~

"I don't need someone to lift me out of the tub," Julian said.

He couldn't believe the look the owner of the boarding house gave him. The minute he came in the door, she'd got-ten flustered. Rubbing her raw hands in her apron, her gaze kept falling to his leg. Caught staring, she turned a richer shade of red. But she wasn't so embarrassed that she couldn't tell him the rules of the house.

"I've got a lot of work to do, so I can't follow around after you," she said. Fidgeting with her apron again, she tilted her head at a stiff angle. It was like the only way she could look him in the eye was to contort herself. "I'll do your wash, but that's extra. Haven't got a special menu for invalids, but . . ."

"I'm not an invalid!"

She inflated when he raised his voice. "And I expect to be treated right. I'm not your mother. You're not paying me enough to tolerate sass."

Vaguely ashamed, Julian dug into his pocket and produced a five-dollar bill. He flattened it on the counter and pushed it toward her. "Sorry, Mrs. Bartow. It's been a long trip; I'm tired."

"Aren't we all?" she asked, plucking the money from his fingers. She rummaged in a cash box beneath the counter but returned a key instead of his change. "Come back Friday if you want your money, or leave your laundry in a bag outside your door. It makes up the difference."

Julian took the key with a nod. Even though the boarding house had tiled steps that led upstairs, he followed Mrs. Bartow's directions down the main hall. From an open door, he caught a glimpse of a pretty boy shouting lines from *Hamlet* at a mirror. Foreign words drifted though a closed door, along with the scent of boiled cabbage.

Then a little rubber ball rolled into the hallway. Julian set his bag down and leaned over to claim it.

"Hey there, could you?"

A thick-faced man stood in the doorway, a baby squirming on his shoulder. He was anchored by a toddler at his ankles. She stared at Julian's crutch as he returned the ball.

"It won't hurt you," Julian reassured her.

"Thank you, lad," the man said as he nodded at the toddler. "She doesn't know any better."

Julian backed into the hallway again and tipped his head toward the man. "No harm done. Suppose we'll be neighbors. I'm Julian Birch."

"They don't hardly cry at all," the man swore. "Cyril Kiedrowicz. Pleasure."

With a nod, Julian left Mr. Kiedrowicz to his children and finally found his room. Unlocking the door, he swung it open slowly to take it in. It was dark, with plain plaster walls and an ugly rag rug. Folded linens sat on the foot of the bed. There was a bare electric lamp, a small table and chair, and a bureau for his things.

Not that he had many. A change of clothes, his pocket

watch, and a little amber piece of rosin. He didn't own his own fiddle, and he wasn't about to steal Dad's when he left. But it bothered him to leave music behind completely.

So he'd slipped the rosin in his satchel. He liked to rub his fingers tacky on it; its warm scent comforted him. Taking off the satchel, he tossed it onto the bureau. Then he took in the whole of the room.

It wasn't much. It didn't smell like spiced apples, and the window let in very little light on account of the building next door.

But for now, it would do. Julian hung his crutches on the hat hook, then his newsboy cap right after. Putting himself to work, he unfurled the linens and made the bed. Rough sheets whispered under his hands. Instead of sunshine, the bedclothes smelled of lye soap. Even the scent burned. When he was finished, Julian opened the window.

At first, there was a hint of flowers on the breeze that slipped into the room. Warm oil and tar followed — not unpleasant, but definitely not like home. Julian heard snatches of conversations from the street. Falling back onto the bed, he tucked his hands beneath his head and listened.

"A million dollars. Can you even imagine?"

"I'm thinking I should powder my face and head down to

First National. If Chaplin's worth a million, I'm worth a thousand at least."

Julian smiled to hear that, but it faded when new voices floated through his window.

A woman, sharp and angry, tossed out words like broken glass. "I don't care who hears me, Ruth. I'd look Wilson in the eye and say it. Show me a mother happy to send her boy to war, and I'll show you a communist."

Julian felt the faintest pang beneath his breast, one that flared when he stopped to think about his family. His brothers were on their way to that war; his parents sat alone in the white farmhouse.

It wasn't the leaving that gave Julian pause. It was the *way* he'd gone: in the middle of the night. Without a note. And sinfully, stealing the money his mother saved for emergencies. What if the hay cutter threw a tooth? What if Old Joe dropped dead? They needed a horse all year round for the farm to work properly.

Guilt blossomed in Julian until it pushed him off the bed. Grabbing his key and his crutches, he hurried into the hall. Julian almost asked Mr. Kiedrowicz if he had stationery but thought better of it.

"Neither a borrower nor a lender be," Julian heard his mother say, her voice a silky memory in his thoughts.

Mrs. Bartow didn't look happy to see him again so soon. "Something the matter?"

"No, ma'am." Julian shook his head. "Is there any chance I could buy paper and an envelope?"

Suspicion narrowed Mrs. Bartow's eyes, but she opened an unseen drawer. Producing a bit of stationery, she held it out to him. "You can have these, but don't make a habit of it. Sun Drug's right around the corner if you need more."

"I'll head that way after supper," Julian said, and went back to his room.

The lamp table wasn't an ideal writing desk, but it would do. Then Julian realized he didn't have a pencil. Or a stamp. He felt stupid, really — there were so many things he needed, and he'd planned for none of them.

Rather than wallow, though, he decided to fix it for himself. Without any help.

Julian put his hat back on. He locked the door carefully and avoided Mrs. Bartow's dumbstruck stare when he came through the lobby yet again. She'd said the drugstore was around the corner.

Stepping into the sunlight. Julian waited for an opening in the people who walked by, then melted into them.

He was on his own in the city. He would decide when to

wake up and how far he could walk. Dinner was whatever he wished it to be. Unless he wanted to snap beans, he'd never have to snap them again. It was thrilling to be independent, though still tinged with regret.

He needed to repay his parents. Only then could he celebrate his freedom without reserve.

Ten

Rolling the quarter between her fingers, Kate jerked her head up when the door finally swung open.

Black feathers splayed out to fill the room; Handsome stretched his wings and turned in a slow, deliberate way. A crackling sound rolled from his gullet, and then in Mollie's own voice, he said, "Nevermore!"

Mollie ignored him, sailing past in a merry flash. She smelled of pipe tobacco, something sweet and roasted. Spinning round, she laughed and dropped herself into the chair across from Kate. With a great, satisfied sigh, she sprawled back. "I'm home!"

"So I see," Kate replied.

"Cheer up, you!" Unsnapping her purse, Mollie pulled

out a bundle wrapped in paper and pushed it toward Kate. "I swear, I had a miserable time without you, so I brought you a treat."

Kate touched the packet; the slightest warmth radiated from it. "What is it?"

"Half my steak and potato. It's delicious. And!" Mollie dug into her purse again. This time, she emerged with two dollar bills. Brushing it against her own nose, she smiled behind them, as if they were a fan and she, a debutante. "To see myself home. Isn't that dear?"

Curiously numb, Kate stared at the money. "That's a lot for a ride home."

"It was for a cab, not a streetcar. I told them they couldn't escort me." Mollie tugged Kate's sleeve playfully. "You know how our imaginary ma loses her temper and beats us when she's drinking."

"Mmm." Kate couldn't find it in herself to go along. "Where did you go?"

Mollie hopped up to change. "Oh, here and there. I let them buy me dinner; they insisted on a couple of dances. Nothing terribly exciting."

Quiet, Kate picked at Mollie's wrapped leftovers. It's not as though they were starving. Hot dinners every night, so far; muffins in the morning, and whatever struck their fancy at work. True, most of what they ate at The Pike was garbage, but ice cream and hot honeyed peanuts made for a delicious lunch all the same.

The steak didn't even smell good, Kate decided, and pushed it away. "I thought we were in this together."

"What?" Mollie started to undress, smiling in disbelief. "We are! That's money in our bank and a dinner we don't have to buy."

Kate didn't say anything. Her head and her heart and her belly were a chaotic jumble. She stared at the floor, listening to the whisper of crêpe de Chine.

"Don't be cross," Mollie said as she shimmied from her skirt.

"I'm not."

"I couldn't take you." Untying her dress shield, Mollie studied Kate's face. "It wouldn't have worked, I'm sorry. You can't string a man along when you've got a chaperone."

"I didn't *want* to go."

As if she hadn't heard Kate at all, Mollie said, "Honestly, I couldn't have. You need a dress. I think I saw a sale sign this morning. Where was it?"

"I don't *want* a dress," Kate snapped. Acid bubbled over, unpleasant and ugly, burning at the edges. "I didn't *want* to go, and I'm not the least bit interested in carousing with a bunch of sailors!"

"I wasn't carousing!"

Suddenly standing, Kate held out her arm to Handsome. She shoved her elbow at him, trying to force him to climb on. When he rearranged his feathers and stared, Kate told him, "We're going for a walk. Get on."

"You can't pick a fight, then leave in the middle of it."

"I don't want to fight."

"A bit late for that," Mollie said. The strap of her combination slid down her shoulder, and she jerked it back into place furiously. "Why don't you say what you're thinking, Kate? Think I'm a hussy, don't you? I'll have you know, they were both gentlemen of the first stripe and — "

"Yes, well, I didn't want to share you! You're my star and my muse and . . ."

Kate cut herself off, but with considerably less fire, Mollie pressed her. "Your what?"

"Friend." Kate finished, without conviction. "My star and my muse, and my friend. You're the only one I have, you know."

An impenetrable wall sprang up between them, invisible but physical all the same. Turning away, Mollie slipped her arms into her dressing gown and tied it tight. All around them, the sounds of other people's lives filtered into their room. A baby cried, a trumpet played, the same melody again and again.

Sick to her stomach, Kate scooped Handsome up like he was a chicken. Ravens weren't meant to be held, and he protested with long, rattling squawks. He may have been angry, but his realness comforted Kate. She held him close as she went to leave.

"We're buying you a dress," Mollie said quietly. "I think you've forgotten you're a girl."

"I know exactly what I am," Kate said, but the words were muffled against Handsome's feathers.

She let herself out and hurried into the city after dark. Unfortunately, she had nowhere to go, so she planted herself on a bench and sighed. A horse cart trundled by, the pony's shoes echoing hollowly against the pavement.

Streetlights glowed overhead, ringed with halos of moths. The poor beasts struck the glass again and again, trying to get to a flame that didn't even exist.

Finally, Handsome freed himself and flapped up to sit on her shoulder. Pecking at a loose tendril of hair, he croaked right in Kate's ear. "I can talk. Can you fly?"

"No," Kate said. "But I wish I could."

~~~~~~~

In the morning, Julian dropped his letter in the mailbox out front, then crossed the street to start his job search.

The Hotel Alexandria towered over him, all glittering glass and stone. Its lobby was a temple of luxury. Chandeliers glowed overhead, golden light dancing through heavy crystal beads. There were velvet settees, and angular ladies perched on them, deep in conversation.

When Julian passed, they stared — delicately, over their compacts, but that was all right. Julian stared back, at their fingernails. They were painted, some pink, others russet. And polished like apples, gleaming and bright. He'd never seen anything like it.

Waiting in line, he watched a bellboy ride his cart down a carpeted hall. He had the same look Sam wore when he was up to something, and he proved it when he reached the lobby. Hopping off the cart, he suddenly walked with measured steps, all innocence and dignity.

A man in a tuxedo emerged from a side door and turned back to lock it. In his free hand, he waved a top hat. It was beyond Julian where somebody would have to be first thing in the morning dressed like that. Even the president kept to his suit jackets and straight ties most of the time.

"Can I help you?"

Julian hurried to the counter. Even though the concierge looked awfully sour, Julian smiled at him anyway. "I'm looking for work . . ."

The concierge cut him off. "I don't think we have anything at the moment."

"Oh, um. All right. Thanks anyway."

"Have a wonderful day," the man replied, but he didn't sound like he meant it.

Julian headed back outside. To be fair, they didn't have a sign in the window, and mostly, he'd wanted to get a look at the inside of a hotel that fine. Curiosity satisfied, he made his way up the block.

Already it was warm. California didn't believe in easing into a day. This time back home, the dew would have burned off. It would have been the golden hour, with the fields clean and gleaming, before the air turned the barn into a steam bath. Loosening one button at his collar, Julian kept moving and tried not to think about the heat.

A Help Wanted notice caught his eye, and he glanced at the sign above his head. BETTIS SHOES. The door was too heavy to push with one hand, so he backed into it instead.

An earthy rush of leather washed over him, the scent of new shoes rich and unbroken. A salesman came out of the back when the bells above the door jingled, and he stopped short.

"The sign says you're hiring," Julian said.

This time, he saw the eyes flick down a split second

before reaching his face again. The salesman put on a fine smile but shook his head. "I'm looking for somebody to go door to door, son. It's a big case to carry on a good day, and there's a lot of walking up stairs and back down again . . ."

Julian tried to ignore the disappointment settling on him. "I understand. Thanks." His smile lasted until he got outside. He probably should have thought about that — what kind of job it was. Then again, how was he to know unless he asked?

He passed a shuttered barbershop and a drugstore, then stopped at the next Help Wanted sign: ZWEIFEL'S SANITARY LAUNDRY. A spark of confidence lit in Julian. If there was one thing he could do, it was laundry. Lord knew he'd done enough back home.

Ringing the bell at the counter, he tried to hide the crutches by leaning forward. A young woman came to the front, probably not much older than he was. Even though she'd bound her black hair tight, little wisps escaped in a halo round her head. Her face was pink from heat, and beads of water clung to her skin.

"What can I do for you?"

"I'm looking for work," Julian said, but didn't leave it at that. "I know how to scrub on a washboard and crank a wringer. Don't imagine you have clotheslines out back, but I can hang and fold and even iron."

The girl smoothed a hand down her apron and looked into the back. "Well, this isn't like doing the wash at home. It's linens for hotels and restaurants. We've got all sorts of machines. Do you know how to use any of them?"

Julian shook his head. "No, but I'm willing to learn."

"All right, um . . ." She pointed to a chair by the door. "Let me go get my father; he's the one you should talk to."

So Julian did as she said, and out of habit, he slid the crutches under the chair and tucked his bad leg behind the good one. He couldn't see into the back, but he heard the machinery quite clearly. A drone underscored metal banging against metal. At regular intervals, a steam hiss would erupt. In reply, someone yelled. Julian couldn't tell if it was a curse or an exclamation.

Finally, an older man stalked up front. His skin was scalded crimson — not only his face. His arms and hands, too, were raw, and sweat shone through his thinning hair. He got all the way to the counter, then stopped to look Julian over. Drying his arms on his apron, he frowned. "Sadie says you're looking for work?"

Julian stood eagerly. "Yes, sir. And I could start today. Mr. Zweifel?"

"Yeah. How old are you?"

"Seventeen," Julian said.

"All right." Shrugging, Mr. Zweifel turned on his heel. "Come on."

Julian wanted to whoop, but instead, he grabbed his crutches and followed the man back. A blast of wet heat soaked him in an instant, but it couldn't weigh him down. It was a small victory, but sweet all the same.

In the back, a high ceiling rose above a huge room with concrete floors. Boys stood beside a row of belt-turned barrels, laundry sloshing away inside them. Never had Julian seen a barrel that big. He could have climbed into one and had room to spare.

At the end of the barrel row, Sadie hauled soaking linens from one of the open wash barrels. Separating out a sheet, she fed it into the rollers of a monstrous machine. It came out the other side, the water squeezed out of it. And there, another girl snatched it up and hung it on a rack. It had multiple arms, all of them draped with damp linens.

"Grab one," Mr. Zweifel said.

Sliding an arm through his crutch, Julian did as he was told. The rack had rollers, so he could use it as his second support. After each new step, he dragged the rack forward and took another. He didn't move as quickly as Mr. Zweifel, but he kept up all right. Turning a corner, he pushed the rack ahead of him. Then he tucked his crutch under his arm again and waited for more directions.

"What's the matter with you?" Mr. Zweifel asked. He didn't bother with subtlety; he pointed right at Julian's leg.

Everything inside Julian wound tight at once. "I had polio when I was a baby. It's not catching."

Mr. Zweifel put his hands on his hips, considering Julian for a long time. Then he turned his attention to a huge wooden box. It took up an entire wall; chimneys jutted from its top and disappeared into the ceiling. Throwing open the door, Mr. Zweifel said, "The whole rack goes inside."

Heat spilled from the inside of the box, ravenous and dry. Julian dutifully pushed the rack inside. Then he locked the wheels down, as Mr. Zweifel instructed, and stepped out. His hair felt crisped after that, and his clothes burned for a moment on his skin.

"All right, close the door. Lock that, too," Mr. Zweifel said. He pointed to a huge crank on the side. "The belt is broken, so you're doing it by hand. Go for twenty minutes, then pull the rack out with that hook."

Julian pulled out his watch to check the time, then took his place at the crank. "How fast?"

Mr. Zweifel waved a hand at him. "Steady. Make some

noise so the ironers know when the rack is done. They'll come get it, and you can go get more. I don't want anybody back here helping. If you can't do it, I don't need you."

"Fair enough," Julian said. He set one of his crutches aside to lean on the other. Taking the crank in hand, he turned it — not easily, but smoothly. He kept time in his head: *one-one thousand, two-one thousand, three* . . . After a moment, the man walked away, leaving him to crank the dryer on his own.

It was hard and hot, but Julian smiled all the same. He'd found his way west. He'd gotten a place to live; now he had a job. He was his own man, and it felt *amazing*.

~~~~~~

Pushing his chair back on two legs, Caleb considered his cards, then the faces around him. He didn't necessarily get along with all the maintenance fellas, but playing euchre was something to do to pass the time.

Holed up after hours in one of the old green rooms at Clune's, they drank tepid beer and let the call go around the table before someone named trump. A bright ember dangled from Jimmy's cigarette; Oscar kept waving his hand like that would clear the smoke somehow. Every so often, Silas threw out his arms in a long stretch. That maneuver revealed the pistol on his belt, and the fact that he was trying to look at everyone else's cards.

After the third time, Caleb flipped a pretzel at him. "We're not playing for money, so knock it off."

Silas' nostrils flared slightly. "A man can't stretch?"

"Don't you get enough stretching at work?"

Leading with a low trump, Oscar mouthed his beer while he waited for the others to play. He didn't join in the conversation; he didn't during work, either. For a couple of days, Caleb thought he might be deaf. But he turned when somebody called his name, and jumped when Jimmy dropped a box of light bulbs. He simply didn't care to socialize.

Silas cursed and threw the highest trump in the deck. "I don't know why I play with you, none of you. I could be down at Rosie's right now."

Laughing, Jimmy flicked a card in. "Doing what? Peeking in her windows?"

"I'll punch you square in the mouth."

"Let's see you try it." Silas boxed at the air, punching holes through the curtain of smoke. Little swirls of it trailed around his fists, and followed when he swept the cards in the middle of the table toward himself. With a snap, he threw down his next card and said, "That's how I make my money on the side. Pow, pow!"

Washing his mouth with a bitter swallow of beer, Caleb flung in a card. "Then why are you working here?"

"I said on the side."

"Mm hmm." Oscar tossed in his next card and raked.

Rather than let Silas blather on, Jimmy pointedly talked over him. "Where d'ya hail from, Virgil?"

"Annapolis," Caleb said. It was a good lie; easy to remember, and hard to get caught in. Baltimore was close enough that he could answer questions when he ran up on somebody who really did come from Annapolis.

"Bet you miss those crab cakes."

"Not really." Caleb played his card, then rolled out of his chair to get another beer. His boots echoed on the floor, which made everyone go still for a moment. They weren't supposed to be in the theatre after closing. Though they were up two long flights of stairs, and hidden behind the old catwalk, they could still get caught.

Jimmy waited for Caleb to come back to ask, "Why'd you leave?"

Sinking into his seat again, Caleb bared his teeth with an ugly smile. "On account of a girl."

"What'd you do?" Silas fanned his cards. "Get her in a family way?"

Carefully selecting his next play, Caleb tossed down a

jack of hearts and pushed his chair on two legs again. His dark eyes cut through the smoke, seemingly lit from within. There was fire under his skin; it seared through his veins with every heartbeat. "I buried one, and I didn't get to bury the other."

A chill rippled through the room. Jimmy's cigarette hissed, burning away in the quiet. For once, even Silas closed his mouth, because it wasn't so much what Caleb said but the way he said it. Too smooth, too sharp, like a filet knife across flesh.

Oscar flipped his last two cards onto the table. "Sorry, Jimmy, I'm set." It was the longest sentence anyone could remember him saying. And with that, he grabbed his hat and slipped down the echoing iron stairs.

"Guess that's a night," Jimmy said.

He was already out of his chair and cast a funny look in Silas' direction. Caleb simply watched, rubbing his thumb against his bottle's open mouth. It sighed softly, an eerie whisper in the old green room. Jimmy shook his head and hit the stairs alone.

Unperturbed, Silas took another swallow of beer, then gathered the cards. "Couple hands of twenty-one, Virgil?"

Eleven

The room at The Ems had become far too small for two.

Three, counting Handsome. He perched on the foot of the bed and shook his wings out. Switching from voice to voice, he carried on a steady monologue made of a single question. "I can talk. Can you fly?"

"Why don't you shut up?" Mollie muttered.

She'd pulled a chair over to sit beneath the open window. Drawing a needle through silk, she mended her only pair of stockings in silence. Likewise, the night before, she'd spoken only enough to insist Kate sleep on the floor.

Kate didn't know how she felt — the acid etching away at her stomach could have been guilt for upsetting Mollie as much as she had. Or it might have been anger that Mollie misunderstood her so completely. There was an extremely healthy possibility that it was lovesickness of the terminal sort: both revealed and unrequited.

Trying to polish her shoes with coffee and an old rag, Kate stole a look over at Mollie and finally said, "Please don't be angry with me."

"I'm not." Mollie drew her thread out long, then stitched it through again. For such a wonderful actress, she didn't sound the least bit convincing.

Kate dipped the rag in the cold coffee again. "I didn't mean to be awful. You were gone so long, I worried."

"Fine."

Single words fell like shards of ice, precise and frigid. The cold extended throughout the room; Mollie kept her eyes on her mending, and Kate sat frozen on her side of the bed. Only Handsome went untouched. His talons clinked on the brass bed frame as he skittered back and forth, a feathered crab.

"I was thinking," Kate said hopefully "we could probably afford a matinee tomorrow."

Unmoved, Mollie said, "I've got to work. So do you."

Finally giving into frustration, Kate put her shoes aside and slid from the bed. Coming round it, she stood behind Mollie's chair. Clasping her hands together, she leaned down, trying to look her in the eye. "Couldn't we please go back again?"

"I don't know what you mean," Mollie said.

Kate sank to her knees beside the chair. "Tell me about your night out. I'm sorry I didn't listen before; I'd like to hear about it now."

Darning two more stitches, Mollie seemed poised to keep her silence. But slowly, she melted. Turning her head ever so slightly, she narrowed her eyes and asked, "Do you?"

"More than anything," Kate swore.

Mollie folded the stocking over her hand. As if experimenting, calculating, her brows went up, and her lips formed a shape before she finally spoke. It was like she had to devise a test, the solution of which only she knew. "The tall fella, his name was Harold. And it was very unfortunate when he took off his hat. He was handsome until I saw him half-shaved. He had red hair, Kate. He looked ridiculous."

Expectation hung between them, and Kate rushed to fulfill it. "Oh, how disappointing. I can't bear a boy who looks like a skinned rabbit."

"That's exactly what he looked like," Mollie said. She laughed, forgetting to be wary. "Though he was much freer with his money than Ollie was."

Kate nodded. "I knew that straight off. Ollie gave me a

dime, but Harold offered up a quarter. So he paid for everything, then?"

Nodding broadly, Mollie launched into a vividly detailed account of her night out with the sailors. She demonstrated the way each one chewed, critiqued their respective abilities to fox-trot. Distilling the smell of their sweat and the nervous dampness of their hands, she waxed all but rhapsodic about dear Ollie and darling Harold.

When she ran out of things to say, she held up her hands. "So they were perfectly fine, but nothing to get exercised about. That's why I didn't let them walk me home. If they'd been even a little interesting, we could have had them in for a nightcap."

With a smile, Kate glanced around the room. "Something delicious from our imaginary bar."

"Oh, I would have asked them to buy," Mollie said. Taking a deep breath, she slumped in the chair and closed her eyes. "I do still think we should buy you a dress."

Kate's heart sank. "We can't possibly. I have a combination, but I left my corset and my stockings behind. Not to mention shoes and hairpins and the like."

Slowly folding her arms, Mollie turned toward the breeze from the window. "Can I be frank with you?"

"Only if you let me be Harry."

At that, Mollie peeked at Kate. "What?"

"Forget it, it's a joke," Kate explained weakly. She turned her hand over and put it on the arm of the chair. *Take it,* Kate thought as hard as she could. "Go on. What were you saying?"

Handsome cackled, "Come here, pretty boy."

Stuffing her hands under her own arms, Mollie turned to look down at Kate. She didn't accuse or shout, but she was very, very plainspoken. "You *make* things happen. You wanted a star and you found one. You wanted to make a motion picture, and you did. You even willed us to Hollywood in the middle of the night."

Confused, Kate said, "Right."

"Kate, if you *wanted* a dress, you'd have one."

Kate said nothing. Her lips felt cold, and the rest of her flesh entirely numb. If she'd had an argument, she would have offered it. But it was true, completely true, and they both knew it.

The trouble was, she didn't see what was wrong with her suits. She liked them, and the way she looked in them. The way they made her feel. There were no words to explain it, except she never felt at *home* in a dress.

At once, it was obvious Kate had taken too long to craft a reply, because Mollie pitched herself out of the chair. In fact, she nearly stumbled because she refused to put her hand down anywhere near Kate's.

Stepping over her, Mollie put her mending in the bureau and reached for her wrap. "I'm going to see if Rykoff's has any day-old fruit. Do you want anything?"

"I could come with you," Kate said, but she already knew the answer was no. Ridiculously mistimed, she finally thought of a counterpoint to Mollie's point. "I'm still exactly myself, you know. I just like to wear trousers."

Mollie draped the wrap over her shoulders. At the door, she stopped, then seemed to consider whether she had anything else to say. Once she did, there was no gentleness to it at all. "We should pretend we never had this conversation."

With that, she let herself out and pulled the door hard and fast behind her.

~~~~~~

After supper, Nathaniel left the table without excusing himself.

They'd had no visitors to the shrouded house since Kate disappeared, nor had they invited any. Consequently, the thin whip of a man walking past their windows was wholly unexpected. And unwelcome, as he curled his hands over his eyes to peer inside.

Nathaniel wrapped the air around himself, stepping from

its nothing embrace into the backyard. Traces of wind clung to him, swirls and eddies that tossed his hair and tugged on the square of chartreuse silk in his front pocket.

He cleared his throat, and when the man turned around, he said, "I believe you may be trespassing."

Instead of bolting, the man pulled off his hat. His weary face was worn in, lines dug so deep in his brow and his cheeks that they caught shadows. "You Witherspoon?"

"Yes," Nathaniel said, and out of habit, followed with, "And you are?"

"Byron Foster. I'm looking for my daughter Irene. Sometimes she calls herself Mollie or Kitty."

Suspicious, Nathaniel looked the man over. *Mollie* wasn't supposed to have family; sometimes young people ended up in bad situations when they were on their own. For all Nathaniel knew, this man was a panderer, or worse.

Choosing his words carefully, Nathaniel said, "The name doesn't sound familiar to me."

Hardness slipped into Byron's voice; he didn't accuse, but he threatened on the edge of it. "A couple fellas at the dancehall said she went home with *your* son."

Nathaniel studied his face. He'd painted hundreds of portraits; with concentration, he found notes of symmetry and balance to prove Byron's identity. Eyes the same shade of underwater light, hints of strawberry blond hair mixed with the gray. Still, relation didn't guarantee safety; Nathaniel approached him warily.

"I don't have a son. Tell me about . . . Irene."

With a sigh, Byron dragged a hand down his face. "She's about yea tall, hair's kinda red, kinda blond. Blue eyes, pretty as a picture. The last time I saw her, she was going dancing. Green dress, old shoes . . . This ringing a bell?"

Oh, it was. "Possibly. Could you — "

"The hell with this — did you do something to her?" His rage came on swiftly and purely, without hint of artifice. Not the egoed anger of a man lost of good property. The fire of a man broken for want of his child.

"We've seen her." Nathaniel opened the back door to invite him in.

Byron scraped off his boots and stepped inside. Taking in the mostly sheeted furniture, he shot Nathaniel an uneasy look. "Moving?"

"We were." Nathaniel brushed past him to start the percolator. "Amelia, this is Mollie's *father*, Byron. Byron, this is my paramour, Amelia."

Silvery whispers passed between Amelia and Nathaniel, silent to their guest.

But she told us . . . Amelia murmured into him.

Yes, I know, Nathaniel replied. He turned to Byron and said aloud, "Our daughter Kate befriended her at the dancehall. She told us her name was Mollie and claimed she had no home."

Byron jerked his head back. "What? We live on Juniper Street; own the place outright!"

Nathaniel said, "That's what she claimed."

"That was almost two weeks ago," Amelia said. Dark circles ringed her eyes; she'd bitten her lips raw. Her gaze kept trailing toward the door, as if she expected Kate to walk through it at any moment.

"Well, where are they now?"

"I wish we knew." Nathaniel spooned coffee into the basket, work that convinced his body that he was doing *something.* "They left in the middle of the night, and we haven't heard from them since."

Sitting down heavily, Byron twisted his hat. "They leave a note?"

"I'm afraid not."

Suddenly, Amelia said, "Los Angeles would be my guess. They're probably in Hollywood. They were making a motion picture together; Mollie wanted to be an actress. Kate was the director."

The percolator protested, little tinny sounds, as

Nathaniel screwed it back together. Looking over his shoulder, he said, "We honestly believed she was an orphan. That's the only reason we didn't send her home."

"Irene's wild like her mother." Byron tossed his hat onto the table and sprawled in his chair. "Can't stay put, won't stay down. That's why I let her go out dancing so much. I thought it would get the act-up out of her system."

Entirely sympathetic, Nathaniel leaned against the counter. "Amelia and I talked to the San Diego police. They wired a description to the police in Los Angeles. The next step will be ads in all the papers, perhaps a private detective."

"She's done this before, run off on me. Like her mama, I said." Worry darkened Byron's eyes. He couldn't sit still either; picking his hat back up, he turned it in his hands. "Never more than a week before."

"It's probably easier for two of them to get by than one. I don't know if Mollie had any money, but Kate had a bit."

Amelia said, "It's not going to last forever. If they get hungry enough . . ."

Byron laughed wearily. "I don't know about your girl, Mrs. Witherspoon, but mine has a way of getting what she wants."

"Miss van den Broek," Amelia corrected absently.

The percolator started to burble, a merry sound at odds with the conversation. Nathaniel poured two cups of coffee and carried them back to the table. Amelia waved off the cup but reached out to stroke his arm instead.

Nathaniel handed one to Byron, and took a seat. "We're out of milk and sugar; my apologies."

"I won't taste it anyhow," Byron said, and took a sip. "Thank you."

Deep in thought, Nathaniel rubbed his thumb against the mug, keeping the same, slow time as Amelia's fingers on his sleeve. Mollie lied about her family; she lied about having no home. She'd even lied about her real name. He couldn't help but wonder if Kate was a step on Mollie's way to getting what she wanted.

It was easier, so much easier, to blame someone else's daughter for this. He looked to Amelia. *You're thinking the same thing, aren't you?*

I blame you. I blame myself. I blame the world, she answered.

The light shifted in the room, daylight sinking to dusk with the first dangerous streak of sunset. She'd been so good about avoiding it, quick to cover windows. Hurrying to inside rooms at the first call of dusk.

For twenty years, she'd resisted its call. Her strange gift had ruined so many lives and damaged so many others. She hadn't been able to save her dear friend Sarah with it. It had directed a bullet into Thomas Rea's breast.

Once, Amelia had played her gift like a parlor game; now she avoided it entirely.

Though strangely, at night, she dreamt of it. And by day, she ached for it — a homesickness that she alone knew. And at that moment, with Kate missing, a streak of crimson light seduced. It had a voice. It promised her visions of her daughter; it begged her to come look again.

Once more, it whispered. *Just this time.*

Standing abruptly, Amelia said, "Excuse me."

"Yes, ma'am," he said.

Better than anyone, Nathaniel recognized Amelia's sudden shift of mood. But because they had company, he didn't leap up to follow. But he did call after her — into her. *Where are you going?*

Sweeping down the hall, Amelia pulled the pins from her hair. It tumbled down her back, wild and windswept — it transformed her; she looked very nearly sixteen again.

And that's precisely what she had in mind. Locking herself in Kate's room, she threw open the curtains and clutched the windowsill.

Anchored there, she made herself look. She stared into the western sky until tears streaked down her cheeks. The sunset rushed up to meet her, an old, eager friend.

With her last deliberate thought, she told Nathaniel, *I'm going to find our daughter.* And then she was silent.

～～～

First thing in the morning and at the end of the day, horse carts pulled up to the laundry. Everyone but Julian and the girls on the manglers would leave their posts to carry fresh, folded linens to the carts for delivery.

Shirt soaked through, Julian kept cranking the dryer. At night, his shoulders ached something fierce, and it took a while for his back to straighten out when he went to bed. He couldn't even claim to like it, because it hurt like hell. But he didn't have it worse than anybody else, and he had a pay packet to look forward to at the end of the week.

Sadie darted past him. She was steamed through like everyone, her clothes gray and damp, but she smiled all the same. Instead of hurrying to the front, she lingered. Her dark eyes trailed over Julian, the smile going crooked.

"It took *two* of us to keep that dryer going before my father hired you."

Shaking his head, Julian said, "Which two?"

Up on her toes, Sadie squinted, then pointed out the girls working the hand-crank mangler. They weren't more than ten years old, responsible for pressing the fabrics too delicate for the automated machines. "Stella and Dottie, right there."

"So I can do the work of a couple of little girls."

"Only just," Sadie said.

Mr. Zweifel bellowed from the front of the laundry, and Sadie scurried away. Prickling with awareness, Julian glanced at the folding table each time someone walked by.

All the faces were familiar now; he'd even started to learn their quirks. Claude bent at the knees for each lift, as if the sheets were lead. Virginia liked to take two stacks at once and pin them securely beneath her chin.

They looked like ants, Julian decided. Invading a picnic and liberating bread crumbs for a feast.

Sadie returned and took her time at the folding table. Balancing laundry on a jutted hip, she didn't seem to notice how it tightened her dress and apron against her waist. It was a tantalizing hint of her, and it caught Julian's eye as easily as the glass pin in her hair did.

Wandering closer, she teased, "There you are again."

"Surprise," Julian said. He guarded the blooming warmth beneath his skin, still counting off seconds to keep his pace on the crank. The rest of his attention was fixed on Sadie and the curl that escaped her chignon to kiss her neck.

"Let me ask you something." Sadie shifted her bundle and took a step closer. "Are you the one I hear singing?"

"I didn't know I was that loud."

Shifting her weight from foot to foot, she looked at him from beneath her lashes. Steam hissed overhead, scrubbing the words away before they could linger. "You're not. I traded Pearl for her spot on the floor. I can hear you fine when I'm racking."

The heat offered some advantages: it hid the blush that crept up Julian's neck. "Have any requests?"

Claude veered away from the table to bump Sadie from behind. "Your dad wants you," he said. Then he grunted beneath a double stack of towels and trudged away with them.

"I'll be right back," Sadie said.

Watching her go, Julian wondered how much nerve he had. That night in the barn with Elise was still fresh. But maybe Sam was right; maybe he'd waited too long to say something.

All along, he'd counted on what things *felt* like with Elise. He'd always figured their hearts were in the same place. If he'd asked what she was thinking —

"Daydreaming?" Sadie asked.

Julian looked up and decided he had all the nerve in the

world. "Thinking about my day off. I heard *Cleopatra*'s playing at the movie palace."

Bouncing slightly, Sadie said, "I heard that too."

Maybe not all the nerve, not yet. "Can I tell you a secret?"

With a quirked brow, Sadie hesitated. But she was still smiling when she said, "Of course."

Julian waved her over with a tip of his head. She only took one step, so he motioned for her again. When she got close enough for whispering, Julian made a show of looking for eavesdroppers. Then he murmured to her, "I've never been to a movie palace before."

Laughter spilled out of her. It crinkled her nose and the corners of her eyes; she quickly sobered herself and said, "I'd run from you screaming if I didn't have work to do."

"You wouldn't have to run very fast," he pointed out. Any minute now, Mr. Zweifel would call for her again, so Julian leapt without waiting for the rest of his nerve to arrive. "Would you go with me? In case I get lost, or confused."

Sadie pretended to think about it. "Well, I'd hate to see you lost or confused."

"So you will?"

"I think I will," Sadie said. Then she frowned. "Look at you, your hair's in your eyes."

With a glance toward the dryer crank, Julian asked, "Could you get it for me? I'm a little occupied."

Sadie's smile softened. Shifting her linens from one hip to the other, she approached him. No runaway spark ignited them; she was sweet and shy, reaching up to touch him. Her fingers slid across his skin, rough to the touch, but gentle in their motion.

"Better?" she asked.

Julian hoped he wasn't staring. "Lots. Thank you."

The sound of footsteps split them apart. Sadie turned to see her father striding toward them.

Dripping with exasperation, he threw his hands up. "What's taking you so long today? The drivers are waiting!"

"Sorry, I was talking to Julian." She slipped around her father. Behind his back, she waved to Julian, then stuck out her tongue. She probably would have crossed her eyes, too, but Mr. Zweifel turned around at the last moment. His posture and presence alone shooed her away.

Satisfied his daughter was back to work, he looked to Julian. "Was she helping you?" he asked.

"No, sir," Julian said. He thought it was obvious she wasn't. His were the only hands on the crank. There wasn't room for anyone else to do it, and the batch in the dryer wasn't done yet. "We were just talking."

"When I hired you, I said no help." Mr. Zweifel's stony expression remained unchanged.

"I swear, I haven't asked for any."

Mr. Zweifel answered with a snort. He moved like winter molasses, turning in agonizing precision. One step, and then a second one a moment later — he was done talking to Julian, but not about to leave yet.

Hurrying past her father, Sadie collected the next stack of linens. With her head down, she still managed to catch Julian's eye. Wriggling her fingers beneath the fresh sheets, she smiled at him one more time, then darted from sight.

"No help," Mr. Zweifel said, stepping into Julian's line of sight. "And no talking."

"Yes, sir." No help and no talking; he could do both. At least he hadn't said no looking, because Julian wasn't sure that was possible.

Twelve

Zora reached for the pencil behind her ear, scowling at the column of numbers in front of her.

Neat stacks of receipts and promise notes covered the table. They ringed the oversize ledger like spectators at a boxing match. It was a fairly violent match at that, because she was trying to find the money to hire a farmhand.

Flipping a scrap of paper, Zora copied a few entries from the ledger. The pencil slipped down the rows as she worked the arithmetic again. One column, then the next, the numbers played peekaboo until the sum revealed itself.

Since Charlie's wife was in earshot, Zora cursed under her breath instead of aloud.

"Everything all right, Mother Birch?" Marjorie asked.

Back stiffening, Zora had to paste on a smile. As a matter of fact, *nothing* was all right.

All her sons were gone and she had no reassurance that any of them were safe.

The asparagus had come in, but she and Em could only pick so fast between them. Their tomatoes rotted on the vine, and the alfalfa needed mowing.

And she wasn't nearly old enough to have a daughter-in-law, let alone one that called her *Mother*. What was this, a fairy tale? Was she some cousin to Hubbard, sister to Goose? Those venerable ladies had never gone skinny-dipping, Zora was sure. They hadn't given in to infatuation and chased their husbands down in a field of wildflowers.

Not that she would ever say such a thing to Marjorie, who was mild and quiet and doing her best. Zora painted on a bit of sweetness and said, "Everything's fine. But if you're wondering about that million dollars we don't have, we still don't have it."

"Blame the bank." Marjorie said. She spooned chow-chow relish into the last Mason jar, then capped it with a lid. The relish's tangy scent lingered in the kitchen, but the steam from the double boiler diluted it. "Daddy says that the First National Bank of His Mattress is the only institution he trusts with his money."

Zora waved the pencil at her. "I don't know about that. I get excellent dividends from the Laundry Basket Savings and Loan."

Amused, they both went back to work until footsteps sounded on the porch. Leaving the ledgers on the table, Zora walked to the back door, then murmured in surprise.

"Josephine Regan, what *are* you wearing?"

Most of the time, Josephine was the fashionable creature who played the organ at church on Sundays. She'd graduated with Charlie and Marjorie, then married two weeks later. It wasn't so small a town that everyone knew everyone, but they all knew Josephine.

When patriotic buntings went up to celebrate the Fourth of July, Josephine was the one who put them there. Anyone ill, elderly, or infirm in Connersville could expect to get a casserole plus a dinner plate from her at some point in time. She sewed all her own clothes from McCall's patterns and made extras for the factory girls who couldn't afford anything extraneous. There was no civic celebration too small, no potluck too large, no need so obscure that Josephine Regan couldn't find a way to make herself useful in it.

At this particular moment, however, she wore a bulky blue uniform and a massive canvas bag at her hip. Though it had to be heavy, Josephine bore its weight proudly and smiled. "I'm delivering your mail, Mrs. Birch."

Marjorie abandoned the canning for a moment to come look. Laughing in surprise, she covered her mouth with her hand, then turned back to look Josephine over. Though completely incredulous, Marjorie couldn't hide her delight. "Did you steal that?"

Sorting through the bag, Josephine shook her head. "Of course not. Mr. Travis got word from the postmaster that he could hire ladies to run the routes."

"And you applied?"

"Obviously." Josephine's nose crinkled, then she added, "It's only while the war's on. They won't need us once the boys come home."

Marjorie leaned against the door. "Does Hugh know?"

"Oh, no. No, he'd never have it," Josephine said. Producing a bundle of letters from the bag, she thumbed through them one by one. "But he's on the Italian front right now, and the house is lonely without him. I thought . . . why shouldn't I?"

"Why shouldn't you, indeed?" Marjorie laughed.

It was like they'd forgotten Zora was there. So she returned to the farm's books. Though numbers never lied, she was determined to rebalance them until they did her bidding. There *would* be money for a farmhand.

"Goodbye, Mrs. Birch," Josephine called. She waved through the screen door before bounding down the steps.

Wheeling round, Marjorie sorted the mail as she approached the table. Suddenly, she squeaked, a soft, startled sound that drew Zora's attention. Hurrying over, Marjorie started to hand over a letter, but then snatched it back. Breathlessly, she said, "It's from Julian."

From Julian. From. Not *about* — not that Marjorie could have known a letter was about him without opening it. The wild, pounding rush of Zora's heartbeat made her feel a bit dizzy, but she thrust out her hand. "Let me see it."

"Oh, Mother Birch, you're not going to faint, are you?"

Taking the letter, Zora valiantly resisted the urge to roll her eyes. She tore the envelope open. It smelled like Julian, the air inside the envelope, the paper filling it. Pressing it to her nose, Zora breathed it in. He was alive, still alive, and out there somewhere!

Unfolding the letter, Zora blinked when a bundle of ten-dollar bills fell to the table. Picking them up quickly, she folded them in one hand and shook the letter out with the other. Julian's handwriting had always been questionable at best, but Zora had never been so happy to try to decipher it.

"What does it say?" Marjorie asked.

Zora skimmed the lines, the first time to herself. Then, the second time, she read aloud for Marjorie's benefit.

"Dear Mama and Papa, I hope this finds you well. I'm fine; I'm writing from my room in Los Angeles. The weather's fair and the food isn't as good as yours. But I like the city so far, and I'm finding my way around.

"I thought it was time for me to make a go of it on my own. I wasn't ever going to be able to work the farm like Charlie does, and that's his legacy anyway. The last thing I wanted was to be the baby the rest of my life. So I headed out west like you did, and hopefully I'll find my place.

"But I have to apologize. Not for leaving, but the way I did it. I should have said goodbye, and I shouldn't have taken your money. I'm awfully sorry, and I hope you'll forgive me. I'm returning all but twenty dollars of it with this letter. I'll send the rest soon.

"I love you, and I miss you. Please write back when you can."

Zora swept away a tear, waving the letter and the money at once. "He signed it and put in his address."

Marjorie caught her breath. "This is such good news; I'm so glad to hear it."

Leaping up, Zora gave Marjorie a quick hug, then hurried outside. Their farm was a vast expanse in green, but Zora didn't need to cut through the fields to find Emerson. She closed her eyes for a moment, drawing up a ghostly vision of all the water that surrounded her. It ran beneath the earth; it flowed through every living thing growing in it.

And then she pushed. With her mind and her will and her body — a subtle gesture of power. Ripples flowed away from her, through the trees and the corn, along the creek that cut through their land. Pulsing with her heartbeat, her touch spread into the distance.

It was a finicky thing, mastering water and being its mistress. But it was an unmistakable thing too, for those who knew how to read the signs. Drifting into the yard, Zora warmed her face in the sun, and she waited.

The corn turned, the stalks twisting subtly as if stretching toward a new sun. And then a faint tremor passed beneath Zora's feet. It startled the chickens and made the screen door rattle.

At once, Marjorie ran onto the porch. Clutching the rail, she asked, "Did you feel that, Mother Birch?"

"I wouldn't be concerned, Marjorie. I'm sure it's nothing. Why don't you get back to your canning?" Zora shooed her away, and waited. When Em was close enough, when she could feel the amber spark of his presence on her skin, Zora would walk into the fields to meet him.

She'd push him down and kiss him until he pulled the pins out of her hair and let it fall in a veil to cover them both. Whatever else passed between them would pass between them, but it would be beautiful, and alive, and theirs.

They both knew enough to celebrate when they could, because perfect moments never lasted.

<p style="text-align:center">~~~~~</p>

Instead of sharing a seat on the red car with Kate, Mollie sat across the aisle on her own bench. Packed in with a pair of very solidly built ladies, Mollie had to perch on the edge to keep her place. At each stop, she pulled her feet out of the way for new riders, a brief, bright gargoyle.

The awkwardness didn't keep her from craning round to look at boys on the street and men in motorcars. "Oh, look at him," she said, pointing out the front window. "He's a treat, don't you think?"

Kate tugged the brim of her cap and hunched clown. It was savagely hot, and sweat already soaked her clothes from the inside. The rubbish bins at The Pike promised to be especially foul with all their contents being roasted by the heat wave. Lucky Mollie would spend the day bathed in ice *and* couldn't leave well enough alone. Kate muttered, "Yes, he's delicious."

"Even better than the Bicycle Boy, and he was really something. Is it me or is Los Angeles positively packed with beautiful people?"

With a sigh, Kate pulled the hat over her eyes. For three days straight, Mollie had been narrating her boygazing in frighteningly minute detail. There was the soldier who bought a soda for himself and one for Mollie too — he had freckles that probably went everywhere. Then it was the waiter at Apffels Coffee, with his sleepy brown eyes and sensual lips.

The Bicycle Boy was mostly notable for — shockingly enough — the old-fashioned bicycle he rode down the pier. Instead of rubberized tires, it had bare metal ones wildly mismatched in size. The hideous thing sounded like a pail full of marbles as it went, and the boy riding it jounced with each rattle. What Mollie could have found fascinating about him would have filled half a postage stamp. He was nothing more than a novelty.

Kate hoped that pretending to sleep would clamp a hand over Mollie's mouth, but it didn't. It seemed to make her talk louder, in fact. Impervious to the heat, Mollie waved her hands in greater gesticulations with each comment.

"Now, that one reminds me of Leonard." All but swooning into the aisle, she leaned toward Kate. "He gave me my first cigarette and my first kiss. I could never smoke again and be a happy lamb, but necking? Oh my, yes, please."

Stamping her feet and rearranging her meaty arms, the

woman next to Mollie made a disapproving sound. But that did nothing to slow the river of chatter, either. Mollie shot the woman a deadly look, then turned back to Kate.

"Have you ever kissed a boy?"

Nerves frayed, Kate pushed her hat back and looked Mollie in the face. "Loads of them. I love kissing boys."

Only then did Mollie realize her error — as far as the other passengers were concerned, she'd asked a boy that question, and now said boy was going on about the wonders of a very masculine kiss.

"For example, Iskender was a wonderful teacher, he was my first. It was a perfect day, the sky was so blue. We'd had ices — mine was lemon, his was melon. We were sitting under an olive tree with them, and our parents were celebrating. They were so caught up, they had no idea what we were doing. His tongue was cold and sweet — "

"Young man," barked one of Mollie's seatmates.

Kate blinked at her innocently. "I'm sorry. Did you want to tell us about your first kiss?"

"Stop it!" Mollie's dismay couldn't have been written more clearly. Even her golden skin, usually so bright and sunblessed, had turned ashen.

Sliding back into her seat, Kate shrugged. "I'd never liked the taste of melon until then. His sister tasted like anise, and I do have to say I developed a permanent fondness. One bite of licorice and I'm back in Paphos."

"Conductor!"

The woman beside Mollie stood abruptly, waving a hand to call one of the attendants.

Kate stretched across the aisle, asking Mollie with a smile, "Have I ever told you about the boy I dream about? I'm standing on a beach watching the sun go down. Then, like a bolt of lightning, I feel him standing behind me. I turn around and . . ."

"You must do something about this churl at once!" the woman shouted. "There are women and children in this car, and the things he's saying!"

The rear conductor wound his way to them. He put his hand on the back of Kate's seat and leaned over. He smiled tightly, and he cajoled, "Come on, now. Why are you giving this nice lady a hard time?"

Kate smiled. "I'm not. *She*'s having a very easy time of eavesdropping. I can't help what she overhears."

"Please stop." Mollie shielded her face from the staring passengers with one hand.

Infuriated, the woman pointed at Kate. "I demand you eject him from this car at once!"

"I demand you eject her," Kate retorted. She stood up

too, hands on hips and chin raised imperiously. "She's the one causing a commotion."

Now the passengers murmured behind them, a drone that drowned the clatter of the red car as it slowed. They could only speculate about what lewd things had been said, and no doubt their imaginations served them quite handily.

Meanwhile, Mollie tried to compress herself in mortification. Though she could be quite compact when she wished to be, no one could miss her brilliant scarlet uniform.

Pulling the bell cord, the conductor rocked as the streetcar stopped. Then he clamped a hand on Kate's shoulder and marched her toward the front. "If I were your father, I'd stripe your hide."

"No you wouldn't. *My* father doesn't believe in corporal punishment."

"Off!" the conductor snapped.

Catching the handrail, Kate swung around to call to Mollie. "I know you find a man in uniform very distinguished, but I couldn't disagree more. I'd rather kiss an actor six days a week. Twice on Sunday."

At that, the conductor grabbed Kate's collar. He didn't pretend to be gentle. The collar strangled, and only stopped when the conductor physically threw her from the car.

She stumbled in the road, pinwheeling around. A chorus

of angry goose-honks sounded. Nimble black cars swerved around her, so close their wake pulled at her clothes. Leaping back, Kate bounded for the sidewalk. Crackling overhead, the electric wires seemed to taunt her.

Another kind of buzzing ran through Kate, and she threw a hand up to wave as the red car drove away. She was loose-limbed with it and felt dangerous. Then, underneath, there was a pounding of her heart, and a ripple in her belly that left her queasy.

It would be a long walk to The Pike if she couldn't catch another red car, but she didn't care. She was tired of caring; she was exhausted with it. She prayed the developed film would come soon, because *The Lady of Shalott* was their masterpiece. If Mollie could only see the art they'd made together, it would mend things between them. It *had* to.

Trying to cage her distress, Kate suffered the one thought that escaped: There was no such thing as a director without a star.

~~~

Though the heat never ceased, Julian found he enjoyed his job when there was something to look forward to at the end of the day. Instead of singing to pass the time, he sang to get

Sadie's attention. He sang when she rewarded him with subtle smiles.

And he sang to amuse himself while a hired mechanic climbed into the ceiling to fix the belt that would automate the dryer again. Since he couldn't help with the machinery, Julian busied himself at the folding tables.

The long linen swaths snapped like pennants in the air when he shook them out. Much quicker than the little kids at the table, he tried to move from pile to pile so no one would get too far ahead of the others. The littlest ones, who couldn't run a machine, got paid by the piece.

Reaching for the next sheet, Julian stopped when a sharp whistle sounded. Turning around, he saw Mr. Zweifel by his office door. He pointed at Julian with his clipboard. Then, with an exaggerated motion, he beckoned him to come, and walked into the office to wait for him.

"I think he wants to talk to you," Dottie whispered.

Whispering back, Julian said, "I think you're right."

Julian scraped the feet of his crutches on the floor to dry them, then hurried to the office, readying an argument. Mr. Zweifel had told him he couldn't accept any help. He'd said nothing about giving it. And he had to agree it was better to work than to stand idle.

But he didn't get a chance to say any of it. As soon as he

reached the office, Mr. Zweifel handed him an envelope. "A week's pay, plus an extra day so you don't go hungry."

Confused, Julian stood there. "I don't understand."

Mr. Zweifel folded the envelope in half, then tucked it into Julian's front pocket. "Now that the dryer's fixed, I don't have a place for you."

With confusion slowly turning to shock, Julian swung back on his crutches, then forward again so no one could overhear their conversation. "Not at all? No disrespect to you, sir, but you've got five-year-olds ironing in the back. I couldn't do that?"

Firm, Mr. Zweifel herded him toward the front door. "I have them doing the job they can do. I pay them less than I pay you."

"I could take less."

"Boy, I have to keep pace with those fellas in Chinatown. You're in the way now, I'm sorry."

The numbness beneath Julian's skin turned brittle. This was all too familiar. Looking around, he realized everyone in the laundry was watching. They all knew. It was written in the sideward tilt of their eye, coded in the way they spoke without moving their mouths overmuch.

Humiliated, Julian made himself stop looking before he found Sadie among them. He wanted her to be outraged on his behalf, but he refused to find her and shatter that fantasy. She was the owner's daughter, after all. She probably knew this was coming.

"Don't take it too hard, kid." Mr. Zweifel clapped him on the back, then reached past to open the front door for him. "I wrote you a note, a recommendation. You can take it around. Bet you're back in business in no time."

"I did a good job for you. I worked hard."

Mr. Zweifel didn't shove him, but he did nudge. Putting his weight behind the gesture, he backed Julian out the door. "That's why you got the note."

"I'll be back tonight," Julian blustered. "To take Sadie to the movie palace."

His face going hard, Mr. Zweifel did push him then. It was a promise of violence to come. "She's working."

"How about tomorrow?"

"Every night this week." Another push, and Mr. Zweifel walked up on him. He may have been shorter, but he was made of muscle and sinew. Years working the laundry had made a brick wall of him. "And for the rest of her natural-born life. Get outta here while you've got your dignity, fella."

Julian longed to take the punch. He wanted to so badly that he could feel a phantom version of it play out within him. Bone would connect with flesh; hard satisfaction would race through his body with the vibration. But when he raised his hand, it was only to brush Mr. Zweifel aside.

"Give her my best," Julian said as he left.

As if he couldn't leave well enough alone, Mr. Zweifel called after him. "I'm doing you a favor, son."

Julian ducked down an alley so he wouldn't look back. He knew if he did, no good would come of that. Mrs. Bartow was strict about her boarding house, but Julian felt certain she ran a finer establishment than the city jail.

Thirteen

Emerging from the alley, Julian looked up the street one way, then down the other. One path led to Mrs. Bartow's, the other to the unknown. Caging himself inside to bake was the last thing Julian wanted to do, so he walked.

The roaring heat outside the laundry suited his temper. It burned off his sweat, leaving him rough with salt and grit. Walking unfamiliar streets occupied his mind and left no time for ruminating.

At first, he thought he'd look for a new job. Back on the horse and all that; that's what Papa would have suggested. But when a manager at the hat factory said he didn't have any use for a cripple, Julian decided to look some other time. Since he'd started the day not punching somebody, he figured it would be for the best to end it that way too.

So instead, he struggled up steep streets, peering in department store windows and stopping to take in the unfamiliar. There were green spaces full of plants he'd never seen. He bought a paper bag of steamed dumplings from a street vendor, then rode the Angels Flight.

It was a two-track inclined railway, connecting a block at the top of a hill with one at the bottom. That was all — two cars perpetually climbing to Hill Street and descending to Olive.

While he burned his tongue on dumplings, Julian peered at the ornate mansion that flanked the train. It was all round towers and steep roofs, crimson walls interrupted by white columns and pediments. Anywhere that could be ornamented was; a fussy house for a fussy street, Julian decided.

At the end of the ride down, Julian wandered the city. Roasting beef and onions wafted from a nearby restaurant, mingling with horse sweat and grease. Red-striped awnings cooled the sidewalk, and Julian stopped short. He'd found the movie palace, entirely by accident.

Heart sinking, he approached the ticket booth. Brightly painted movie posters promised adventure and romance and thrills. As if to taunt him, a sign reading MUSICIANS WANTED obscured the clerk. Tentatively, Julian tapped the glass.

"Welcome to Clune's Theatre Beautiful," the clerk droned. "I'm sorry to say the matinee's already started. No one's admitted after the first reel."

Julian shifted on his crutches, trying to look past his own reflection in the glass. "When's the next showing, then?"

"Eight o'clock sharp. And like I said, no one's admitted—"

"After the first reel, I know. Thanks." Julian backed away, then thought better of it. Tapping on the glass again, he was the smallest bit pleased to see the clerk frown before masking the expression.

"Welcome to Clune's Theatre Beautiful," he said, unable to disguise a hint of annoyance. "Can I help you?"

Julian pointed at the sign. "What kind of musicians?"

With a sigh, the clerk jerked a thumb. "Beats me. Ask at the manager's entrance on Fifth Street."

But there'd be no point. Thanking the clerk, Julian moved along, newly dimmed. It didn't take two feet to play a fiddle, but it *did* take a fiddle. Buying one was out of the question. He'd paid his room up for a month, but he'd returned the rest of Mama's money. The four dollars and a reference letter in his pocket had to last him.

Julian put his head down and kept walking. The scarlet streetcars clattered as they passed, and it seemed nobody with an automobile could be satisfied without constantly honking their horn. There was no such thing as quiet in Los Angeles, at least, not that he'd found.

Drowning in a bitter rush of homesickness, he glanced at his watch, and then the sun. He hadn't gone to the boardwalk yet; he'd never seen the ocean. Not in person, not for real.

When he'd run away, it could have been to anywhere. Florida, where it never snowed, Maryland, where his grandparents lived.

But he'd headed west — to the romance of jagged mountains and Pacific winds, to a place that promised adventure and excitement. California was supposed to be full of stars and possibility. And it was the only place he could imagine finding the girl he'd seen by magic his whole life.

So he squared his shoulders and drove all else from his mind. Crossing the street, he waited for the next red car. When it arrived, he ignored the conductor's hand. He hauled himself aboard, and chose a window seat for the ride to Long Beach.

He could cool himself in the water and watch the sun set over the sea. Tomorrow he'd worry about a job. That was the plan. Much like his mother's plans, however, Julian's didn't always work out the way he intended.

A bag of popcorn and a bottle of soda were hardly dinner, but then, Kate didn't feel much like eating.

Once the spike of energy from fighting with Mollie had worn off, Kate found she mainly wanted to lie down and sleep. Instead, she'd trudged the rest of the way to The Pike to work her shift.

She avoided the main boardwalk. Every time she saw a flash of red, Kate hid. More than the rancid waft of rotting garbage, the prospect of going back to The Ems made Kate sick to her stomach.

So a sad, cheap dinner it was, and a sad, cheap perch on the beach as evening approached. She could have had *mantou* and *geng* if Chinatown hadn't been three cars away. Or a big bowl of *tagliatelle* close to The Ems. But no, it was fizzy soda and popcorn. At least the popcorn was good for feeding the birds.

Gray-green waves danced in sharp peaks, the swells raising white foam, then swallowing it. Seagulls tossed themselves onto the invisible currents of the wind, shrieking to the heavens.

Staring into the sea, Kate sat on a stone pocked with bird droppings. It was like one of her father's marble palettes — smeared and mottled, but not cold. It clung to its baked heat jealously, like the air did. Pale veins of heat lightning streaked through the clouds, a still-distant storm promising relief.

Kate couldn't cry, but she couldn't stop wanting to, either. She had no home. No one who could help her. Not even a dollar in her pocket to send a telegram to her parents.

They'd probably moved on to New York without her. They weren't staying people. Settling people. They were probably furious, but they were free without her.

When even that miserable thought failed to prime her tears, Kate slid to her feet. The sky stretched out, tied in ashen knots. The horizon was a dark line, threaded between rough waters and churning clouds.

Tossing the last of her popcorn to the birds, Kate stuffed the bag into her pocket and approached the water. If she had her camera, if it would pick up all the shades of dusk around her, she knew what she'd film: Ophelia — not the monologue, absolutely not. Rosemary was for fried chicken, not for remembrance.

But with the *right* Ophelia, Kate would follow her into this ocean. The waves would welcome her, making her gown transparent and then into foam. Down below, her hair would become seaweed, and her skin would turn green — pale and speckled with uncertain light.

The wind picked up. It carried the coming storm, introducing it with the rough, scrubbed-fresh taste of water in the air. Plucking at her clothes, it swept across her throat, insinuated fingers into her collar. The horizon broke, one streak of amber light suddenly flooding through.

Eyes wide, Kate slowly reached for her hat. Pushing aside the clumsy touch of the wind, the familiar, velvet caress slipped over her skin. It kissed the bare back of her neck, and Kate held her breath. She had seen this before, a hundred times before. Everything — every bit of it. Destiny had finally arrived.

Electricity streaked through her, waking every numb bit of her flesh. Everything in her moved automatically; her body knew what to do. She pulled off her hat to let the wind take her hair. No matter that it was caught in pins and loose braids, she turned all the same.

He was there.

~~~~~

She wasn't there. Before him was the sunset, all around him, the scent of honeysuckle, but she wasn't there.

Julian had only enough time to think that before a smooth-faced boy attacked him. A blur of plum wool, he crashed into Julian, knocking them both to the sand. Tangled in his own crutches, Julian struggled to free himself and swallowed shock when the boy kissed him.

Speechless, Julian sputtered. But before he could push him off, the boy's hair suddenly came loose. It looked almost as if it had sprouted, growing by magic in length and in color . . . and there was the silver streak. The wind played it out, tugging curls free, fingering through long waves.

"You're real," the boy — not a boy — breathed. His — her — eyes were dark wells, long lashes fanning against her skin. Amazement lit her from within; she glowed surely as a lantern would. Then she rolled off of him and planted her backside in the sand. "That kiss was *not* what I expected."

Dragging himself back a few feet, Julian said, "Are you crazy?"

She took a deep breath, sinking down as it drained out of her. "Sadly, yes, I probably am. But I'm not imagining you, am I? I didn't accidentally go and drown myself in the ocean, did I?"

Julian stared. Openly, and incredulously. This was the face he'd seen every time he died, and it belonged to a lunatic of a girl in a man's suit. Picking his own hat out of the sand, Julian said, "Alive and well. Well, I'll vouch for alive."

"I'm Kate," she said, crawling closer to him. "You recognize me, don't you? Please say you do."

Wary, Julian pulled his hat back on. The honeysuckle

had faded, leaving the tang of a coming storm in the air. It *was* her, it had to be. He knew the shape of her face and the arch of her brows. Even her lips were familiar —

Blushing, Julian reached for his crutches. "I recognize you. There. Happy?"

Kate scrambled to her feet and offered her hand. "Incredibly. You have to tell me everything. I want to know every last detail. Where you're from, and if you like your bacon chewy . . ."

"Crispy," he said, but he didn't take her hand. Raising his crutches, he planted their feet. Then he hauled himself up by them, trying to shake off as much prickling sand as possible. He already felt it in his shoe, and itching on his neck. "I . . . No offense, Kate, but I don't know what to make of you."

Disbelief lit her eyes, and she walked up to him. "Oh, ask me anything. I'll tell you true. But me first again. What's your name? Is it something mysterious like Rochester? No, no, you don't look cruel at all. You're a Laurie, aren't you?"

"I'm a Julian," he said.

She repeated the name like a fervent prayer. She even clasped her hands together and gazed at the sky. Every bit of her flickered and twitched — to be honest, it exhausted Julian to look at all that animation at once. Then, abruptly, she turned her attention to him again.

"What can you do?" she asked. She circled him, staring like she might be able to see through his skin, right down to his bones.

Trying to follow her with his gaze, Julian said, "What do you mean?"

Kate lunged again, then petted him when he flinched. "I mean, what can you do? I stop time, but only a little bit. Thirty seconds; it's completely useless. What about you?"

Cold swept through Julian. His gift had always been his secret, a family secret. For a stranger, however familiar, to *ask* for it, unnerved him. He'd always believed himself singular. The shock of seeing his mother command water had nearly undone him.

"Can we go back to the bacon question?"

"You already answered that."

"Well, then . . ." Julian looked away, then pointed at her. "How do I know you're telling *me* the truth?"

She blinked at him. "Why would I lie?"

Surprising himself, Julian laughed. It wasn't a mirthful sound by any stretch of the imagination. Pulling out his pocket watch, he pressed the button to open it. The hands ticked along regularly, something solid and real to judge her by. "If you can't do it . . ."

"A little 'you show me yours, I'll show you mine'? All right." Taking his hand, Kate tugged on him, then glanced down. That was the first time she'd really considered the crutches or his leg. Raising her gaze to his face again, she said, "Come on. I don't want to drag you."

Julian had little doubt she'd do it. So he followed her to the edge of the water. Since she'd wondered aloud whether she might have drowned herself, he worried when she closed her eyes.

But instead of pitching into the waves, she exhaled. It wasn't half a breath; she spilled out all the air inside her, it seemed. Toward the end, a faint wheeze rattled in her throat. He moved to shake her, but her eyes snapped open, and she marveled up at him.

"I didn't see you this time because you're here."

"Nothing happened," he said. He turned the watch to her, its slender arms still ticking along.

Scoffing, Kate said, "Well, I didn't stop *us*. That would be useless! Come on, open your eyes, Julian. Put down your stupid watch and look."

It wasn't a stupid watch, and he was about to tell her that. But the protest died on his lips, because he *looked*. In spite of the clockwork still running in his hand, the world stood absolutely still.

A single sea bird hung above them, as if dangling on a line. The ocean rushed neither in nor out. It stood in tiny, chopped peaks, stiff like meringue. Surrounded by an unnatural quiet, they heard no waves, nor wind — nothing but their own breaths. Kate had closed them in a snow globe; the world beyond their orb was a still, empty canvas.

Julian was glad for his crutches; they kept him from falling when his knee went weak. This was an impossible thing. An extraordinary thing. And he could feel it reacting to him. For his entire life, he'd summoned his gift deliberately. It didn't linger or beckon or call.

But at that moment, standing there with her, there was too much inside him. He felt the weight of the world shift; he thought he might split with it. Scarlet lights danced in the dark, some beneath the water, some on the sand.

Even without testing it, somehow he knew that those weren't faerie lights. They were bodies: of fish, and flies, and all the little things on the beach that he could raise with a breath — if he wanted to.

"Well?" Kate asked. "It's something, isn't it?"

Julian could barely feel his own lips when he murmured back. "And how."

In San Diego, Amelia dropped her mirror.

She hadn't spoken a word since locking herself up with the sunset the night before. There were no words, not for the things she'd seen. Hollowed by fire, she'd haunted the house with Nathaniel at her side, comforted when he whispered into her. When he touched her face with rough fingers and kissed her until her breath faltered.

Nathaniel waited; she felt him waiting. Since their first meeting so many years ago, he'd been there. Insubstantial as mist sometimes, nothing more than a kiss of the wind, but he'd been there all along. Every day, she felt his shadow, she knew his presence.

But suddenly, he was gone.

It felt like death, a sudden severing marked only by silence. A dull ache started in her temple when she tried to speak into him. Nothing happened; the words wouldn't form. It was like remembering a melody but forgetting the lyrics. It wasn't a song anymore. It was something incomplete and ephemeral.

Panic sharpened her voice. "Nate?"

No answer came. Knocking over her chair, Amelia knotted her robe and started down the hall. White silk swirled around her; her hair fell in a veil around her shoulders. She could have been a ghost; anyone peeking through the windows would have believed it completely.

A door swung open at the other end of the hall, and Nathaniel stepped into it. He'd never been ungainly; his hips had always rolled with smooth assurance. But now he stumbled as he held out a hand to her. The velvet certainty when he murmured had faded. He sounded as strained as she.

"Amelia?"

Rushing into his arms, Amelia pressed her ear against his chest. His heart beat like the thrum of hummingbird wings, but she still whispered desperately, "I can't hear you anymore. I can't hear you."

"It's all right," Nathaniel lied. He crushed her close and kissed her hair. His hands strayed down the curve of her back. It was almost like he had to reassure himself that she was there.

Because she was speaking again, aloud anyway, he dared a question. "What did you see last night, Amelia?"

She looked up at him. Her lips were pale, bluish in the dark, and bruised shadows filled the hollows of her cheeks. Shaking her head, she stilled when he brushed a thumb along her face.

"You can tell me," he said.

Amelia rose up to whisper to him — into his ears now that she could slip in no deeper. And she spoke with a sibyl's voice, breath crackling as she encompassed the whole of the vision into a single prophecy.

"Last night in the vespers," she said, "I saw the end of the world."

Fourteen

Pulling up her knees, Kate wrapped her arms around them and drank in the stillness. Julian's watch ticked away, and she turned to peer at its face again.

She laughed — delighted, dumbstruck — then told him, "I've never kept it up this long before."

Julian sprawled as comfortably as he could on sand and stone, and watched Kate as if she were an exhibit. The crested Californian girl-monkey — constantly in motion, entirely distractible.

"Is it everything?" he asked. "The whole world?"

Shaking her head, Kate closed his watch. Her hair rolled in long, graceful waves, at odds with the broad shoulders of her suit. "Hardly. It's like a bubble. I can make it as small as myself, but so far, no bigger than a house."

"Then what would happen if someone walked by? Do we look like statues to them?"

"No." Kate slid the watch chain between her fingers, passing the watch from hand to hand. "Daddy says I disappear. There one minute, then gone. That's what it looks like when he goes on the wind, too."

"I still can't fathom that."

"Why not? Don't you have an imagination?" Quickly, Kate added, "Don't take that the wrong way."

"How should I take it?" Julian asked with a frown. "It's not a compliment."

"It's not an insult either."

"Maybe not where you're from!"

Kate sighed at him. "You're changing the subject. Do you want to know how it works or not?"

Exasperated, Julian said, "Dying to. Enlighten me."

"Well, Julian Sarcastic, all you have to do is hold on. He calls the wind, and it swirls all around. It gets dark, and there are stars everywhere, gold ones. You know you're moving, but it's more a sensation. And then it stops, and you're somewhere else completely."

"Like that, huh?" Julian asked, and this time, he restrained the sarcasm.

"Yes! Well, sometimes we crash into rivers. Daddy can't

cross water, we don't know why. Mimi fell in one once. It was hilarious!"

It was too fantastic by half, but Julian was too polite to call her a liar. Still, he knew for an absolute truth what he could do. He'd seen what his mother managed with a cup of water. The endless fields of grain at home testified to his father's gift. He replied as diplomatically as possible. "Sounds like a pain."

"It is." Kate opened his watch again, gazing down at its face. Fifteen minutes had already passed. "We have to walk around lakes and rivers and creeks. Or through them. Or find a boat? In any case, forget going long distances. I've spent half my life on the White Star line."

That watch was the one fine thing he owned, and Julian didn't want to gum it up with sand or too much jostling. Gently, he reclaimed it and threw in a question to distract her. "So why you? Why do you get to beat Father Time?"

Kate crawled to him and dropped her head in his lap. "I told you, the elements favor us. Fire for Mimi, air for Daddy."

Her hair spread in a wide fan, flowing over his legs and across the ground. The silver strands twined together. Swirling and sweeping toward him, they looked like a horn. Warmth radiated from her; she felt vital, substantial.

Strange currents warred within Julian. She was too

familiar; she touched him too easily and confessed too much. At the same time, he wanted to pull her ears and measure her feet against his own.

Since he couldn't decide where to put his hands, Julian finally tucked them under his arms. "Time isn't an element."

"Aether is," she replied. She pressed a fingertip to his nose. "That's what you get when you mix all the elements together. The heavens. The breath of gods."

Staring at her openly, Julian couldn't think of a thing to say at first. The only ether he'd ever heard of was the kind Doc Smith used to knock his patients out. It burned to breathe, and when you woke up, whatever tooth had bothered you was pulled clean out.

Finally, Julian said, "God breath."

"Not 'I'll huff and I'll puff' breath, Julian. Honestly." Kate rolled her eyes. "I mean the breath that creates everything. *Quintessence.* And you're changing the subject. Again."

True, he was. Mostly because the subject was absolutely mad. Trying reason with her, he said, "But you're not all four mixed up. Fire and air, one plus one equals you."

"But you plus me," she said. She must have realized Julian still hadn't confessed his magic, because she righted herself immediately. Standing on her knees, she wobbled toward him. "Ohhh, you have elemental parents!"

Reflexively, Julian shook his head. His parents' secrets of water and earth weren't his to tell.

Kate studied his face. "You still haven't told me what you can do."

"Maybe there's nothing to tell."

"Of course there is. If there weren't, you would have said so." Kate smiled proudly. "You keep avoiding the question, which means there is."

The logic was suspect, but Julian couldn't honestly say she was wrong. Looking toward the ocean, still frozen, the seagull, still dangling, Julian shook his head. "I don't know if I should."

Kate answered that with a look. One brow arched, her lips pursed, she kept her silence until it stretched out so long, Julian replied to make her stop.

"All right. But I'm warning you, if you scream . . ."

"Why would I scream?" Kate asked. "Is it disgusting? Can you take off your own face?"

Shuddering, Julian leaned away from her. "No!"

"Oh." Sinking down again, Kate frowned. "Well, quit making me guess and do it. I'm going to be disappointed now. I should have liked to see you with your face off."

If he had no imagination, Julian believed Kate had entirely too much. Planting his crutches, he pulled himself up.

Already, his gift stirred in his blood. It cleared his eyes and, uncommanded, revealed the scarlet lights on the beach again. Some cast a blinding glare; others hardly glowed at all.

Choosing the brightest, closest spot, Julian raked the sand with the foot of his crutch, then pointed down. "Pick that up for me?"

Eager, Kate bounded over. But her smile faded when she scooped up a handful of sand crowned by a dead turtle. It was no bigger than a quarter. Standing with it, she asked uneasily, "This poor thing?"

"Yep."

"But he's dead," she murmured.

"I know." Reaching out, Julian made her raise her hands. Pale sand streamed between her fingers. The little turtle didn't move at all, even when Julian righted it. It sat on its dwindling cairn, a perfect deceased specimen.

He felt Kate watching him, even without raising his gaze. His own heart sped, an anxious warning. He'd never let anyone outside his family see this.

"Are you doing it?" Kate whispered.

The question prickled; of course he wasn't doing anything yet. But rather than argue, Julian drew a breath, and then blew.

He was suddenly too aware of the stillness around him. With the wind and waves conquered, no birds crying out, no beachgoers laughing, the only sound between them was the whisper of his breath, and that went on and on.

It burned as it drained from him. Before it was exhausted, the turtle thrust its head from its shell. Four tiny feet followed, scrabbling around for purchase. Kate's eyes widened, and she dropped to her knees. Not to pray but to set the turtle free.

Tensed, Julian waited for the darkness to come. The turtle was such a small thing, he believed it would be a blink, a nod of his head, and then an escape from the nothing place. He buzzed with anticipation. What would he see, now that the girl with the silver lock stood in front of him?

But the dark never came. He waited for it, all but courted it. Still, he stood there, watching the turtle escape the edge of Kate's bubble. She hadn't lied — or her father had been an honest reporter. One moment, the turtle was there, and when it breached the edges of the spell, it was gone.

Almost exultant, Kate shook his arm, then spun away. Her face glowed, and her laughter echoed all around. "I've never wanted to faint more in my life," she said. "Stars and garters, Julian, that was *spectacular!*"

Zora stood in the barn's loft door, watching the eastern sky turn shades of purple and night.

She never had learned to love the sunset, but twilight held its own impeccable delights. It trailed an invisible hand over the corn, its touch whispering between the stalks. Night-blooming flowers opened at its call.

And twilight always saw Emerson walking home, his hat a dark spot that moved through the fields.

From the loft, Zora spotted a ripple among the rows. Leaning against the wood frame, she rubbed at the warmth in her breast. It was tender pleasure, that she could still be infatuated with her husband, even after four sons and twenty years.

But then she frowned, because the tremor beneath her feet didn't come.

The pleasure drained away. She didn't know what a stranger was doing in their fields, but she didn't like it. Boots thumping on the ladder as she climbed down, Zora grabbed the closest pitchfork and stalked outside. Her hair, already half-loose from a day of work, broke free in unruly waves around her face.

"I'd go right back where you came from, if I were you," Zora called.

No one answered, so she hefted the pitchfork with authority. Lights from the kitchen outlined her; her shadow cast long and dark across the lawn. A man emerged from the field, and Zora swallowed a yelp. It wouldn't do to sound afraid; the only way to handle intruders was confidently.

"Zo?" Emerson asked, pulling off his hat. Bafflement marked his brows, but he took slow steps — probably just in case. When his wife wielded a weapon, she was a dangerous creature indeed.

Slowly lowering the pitchfork, Zora said, "Em? You snuck up on me."

Relieved, Emerson flipped his hat toward her, then followed after it. "Looks like."

Zora put a hand up, intercepting him. Her palm skimmed his arm, its familiar shape comforting and warm. But she went a little cold inside, repeating more emphatically. "You snuck up on me. How?"

It was an excellent question. Emerson's tremor always announced him; he'd told Zora once that he heard the whisper of new snow whenever she came near. They'd always known Julian would have some gift. From the moment he was born, he added a low, electric sort of hum to the house. When he left, the hum fell silent. And now, something else had fallen silent, too.

Slipping an arm around Emerson's waist, Zora exhaled and gazed into the dark. No ghostly waves rose up, though she knew every stream, every well, every puddle on this land the way she knew the freckles on Emerson's shoulders. She called to the water, but the water had no answer.

Zora murmured, "Make the corn turn."

Rippling beside her, Emerson moved in subtle ways. But the corn stood straight, disinterested in his mastery. Stubborn, Emerson tried again, waving a hand as if their magic had ever required more than will. Her touch gentle, Zora reached out to catch that hand and pulled it to her lips.

A kiss for his dusty skin, and Zora gazed up at him. "It's gone, isn't it?"

"Looks like," he replied.

Grief, the thinnest ribbon of it, wound through her. Whatever strange providence had granted the gift had reclaimed it. All the glorious details of it, being able to call to Emerson through the fields, to feel him coming home to her — that she would miss.

But a weight lifted too — the fear that one day she would simply become water and drain back into the sea had dissipated. No more would she worry that Emerson would walk into his fields and never emerge, made one with the land that sustained them.

The ache lingered, and she asked, "Are you all right?"

"We'll get by, Zo. We always have."

Moonlight brushed the age from his face; it smoothed the lines and freckles wrought by long days worked in the sun. Nothing would bring back the softness he used to have in his features.

But for a moment, he was exactly the sooner who'd stopped his buckboard in the middle of the night for her. The boy who'd played waltzes that broke her heart, who'd met her at the river to make her heart whole again.

Zora pressed her cheek against his hand and sighed. "You're probably right."

"Probably?" Emerson tugged her hair, then dipped her back for a kiss. "That's the best I get?"

Looping her arms around his neck, she said, "Unless you earn more."

At that, Emerson swept an arm beneath her knees and picked her up. He hefted her easily and took advantage, kissing her lips, her chin, her throat. He didn't try to carry her home, those days were past. But the thrill was ever the same, at least until he arched an eyebrow at her.

"How's that, *Mother* Birch?"

"I'm glad you think you're funny," Zora said. She wriggled out of his grasp and backed toward the house. "You're the only one who does."

And then she ran; not as fast as she used to, but he

couldn't chase as fast as he used to either. They let the things they'd lost peel away, left behind for the life they still lived.

They had a homely supper in the kitchen, and afterward, Zora insisted that Marjorie play the piano along with Emerson's fiddle.

Once the night settled, Zora took out two sheets of her best stationery. Flipping to the *V*s in her address book, she smiled. Beneath Amelia's name, she'd crossed out so many addresses over the years. It was a map of World's Fairs, kept in her own neat hand. Paris, Norfolk, Turin . . . and lately, San Diego.

Pondering a moment, Zora finally wrote:

> *Dear Amelia,*
> *The elements have moved on from our house, and I wonder if they've abandoned yours, too. Julian left home to find his fortune, and now Em and I find ourselves ordinary. Perhaps they're connected. Katherine's too young yet to leave, so I may be writing to warn you. How funny that I put pen to paper to tell your future for once.*

An answer came by telegram, two days later.

KATE MISSING. MAGIC TOO. ALL IS LOST.

How many people could say they'd seen a miracle?

Kate spun around, then ran back to Julian to marvel at him. Planting both hands on his shoulders, she stood on her toes to look him directly in the eye. She couldn't stop smiling, not that she wanted to at the moment.

"You're amazing," she said, experimentally moving her hands until she felt his pulse. It didn't race nearly so fast as hers, which was a shame. "Is it only animals? Could you revive a person? What if they were dismembered, could you put them back together?"

Gingerly, Julian covered her hands with his own and said, "You have a diseased mind."

"But that doesn't answer the question," she replied.

"I don't know, Kate." Julian peered down at her, like he was examining a particularly unusual discovery. "Could you only stop time on half a person? Would they look like you'd sawed them in two?"

Pleasure threaded through her, embroidering her enthusiasm. His hands were rough and too warm, but they kept her — he kept her. Instead of pulling away, she pressed closer. He smelled like sunshine and soap and some alien spice she couldn't place.

Swaying against him, she said, "I never thought of trying before. Now I have to!"

With a helpless laugh, Julian surrendered. Grasping her arms, he pried her off of him and said, "Let me know how that goes. You probably can now. You made my gift go funny, so why not yours?"

Offended, Kate asked, "Funny hilarious or funny bizarre?"

"Mostly bizarre. I usually have a spell after I do that. I usually can't see a . . . a spark left in something. And you've kept us stopped for a lot more than thirty seconds."

Tipping her head back to consider that thread of lightning, that still bird, she had to agree. She wound around him again, marveling. All her life, her gift came with that flash — that glimpse of him. And now that he stood before her, her magic was wild and free. "It's the two of us. We were meant to be together."

Though he was gentle doing it, Julian peeled her off again and held her at a distance. "I don't know about that."

When he released her, Kate collapsed on the inside. They'd been having such a good time together. She'd met a world's worth of people with elemental graces, but Julian was the first one like *her*.

He didn't fit either — his gift was a breath too. She wanted to peek in his pockets, and look into his ears. Hungry for his details, she'd thought of a legion of questions to ask him. If they went unanswered, she thought she might die.

And less dramatically, though she hated to admit she was being dramatic, if he left, she'd have to go back to The Ems. There was nothing there to recommend it at the moment; Mollie waited to ignore her.

Except, of course, to insist that Kate keep her pallet on the floor instead of sharing the bed. A whispered ache ran down her spine. The floor was hard, and the carpet smelled of formaldehyde.

Much more sober than before, Kate asked, "All right. So, you're leaving?"

"It's late," he said. "I've got to find a new job tomorrow."

"What happened to the old one?"

Julian's eyes darkened. "I lost it. Doesn't matter."

There was a story there, she could tell. But he looked stony enough that she decided it was a story for another time. If there would be another time.

Sweeping her hands beneath her hair, she caught the whole length of it. "I'm sorry."

An unreadable expression flickered through his brown eyes. Then he lifted both legs and dangled between his crutches for a moment. "Not your fault. It turned out all right. I finally got to meet you."

Maybe things weren't so dire after all. Smiling, Kate said, "Excellent silver lining, Julian. But I have a really important question."

"It better not be about decapitation."

"Why, do you know something about it?"

Groaning, Julian started to back away. "Important question, Kate?"

"We're going to see each other again, aren't we?"

Inwardly, Kate groaned at how pitiful she sounded. She would have needed to fall to her knees and cradle a dying, three-legged puppy, in the rain — no, in the *snow* — and possibly cough a delicate plume of blood into her dirty handkerchief, to come across more pathetic than she just had. It was embarrassing, and awful, and —

"I'm not even gone yet," Julian said. Then, in disbelief he said, "You didn't think I was gonna let you walk home alone?"

Taken aback, Kate nodded, but not too hard, because he already looked awfully offended. "You might have."

"I never would," he said.

Curling her toes in her shoes, Kate bounded over. He wasn't going away! She still had time to unravel all his mysteries. Or some of them. As many as she could on the long trip back to The Ems.

Since he needed his hands for his crutches, she took hold of his sleeve. "What about after you walk me home? Will I see you after that?"

"Depends on what happens between here and there."

It took her a moment to realize he was joking. Under her breath, she muttered a fond insult in his direction, then tugged his sleeve, leading him out of her little bubble of time. She didn't know how to turn it off — it had always stopped on its own before.

"Come on. I don't want you turning into a pumpkin on me."

"What does that even mean?" Julian laughed, then the spark went out in his eyes.

As they stepped through the borders of Kate's magic, cold rushed around them, and Julian fell.

No — he dropped.

Because he didn't put out his hands or try to catch himself. Crashing into the sand, his body flopped like a doll's. It came to rest in an awkward curve, one arm bent behind him, the other thrown over his head.

"Julian!" Kate cried, and lunged after him.

She shuddered because he felt like warm jelly under her

hands. His head lolled from side to side, his eyes half-open but fixed. It was unnatural, how boneless he was. How *still* he was. The wind, newly started, swept between them. Overhead, birds shrieked once more, but Julian had stopped. Completely.

Pressing her ear to his chest, Kate heard nothing. Her panic rising, she thumped his breastbone, as if that might make his heart reply. Bodies were forever making strange noises, usually at embarrassing times. They weren't meant to be hollow shells. They shouldn't echo.

Even as she covered his mouth with her hand, trying to find his breath, some little proof that he lived, Kate screamed for help. But there was no one to hear it.

The beach was deserted. Even the glass bulbs on the boardwalk had gone dark. Made darker still by the strangely moonless sky. It was awful and beautiful — entirely cloud-less, and pierced with a million silver stars.

Ignoring the sharp hitch in her chest, Kate stood. There had to be a police call box nearby. This was more than she could handle on her own. Jumbled, her thoughts urged her to go. At the same time, her stomach clenched at the prospect of leaving Julian alone. He looked so helpless.

His eyes opened.

In terrible succession, he drew a rattling breath

and began to shake. Quivering became thrashing. Joints cracking, Julian clawed deep furrows in the sand. Twisted in an unnatural arch, he gasped and collapsed.

"Julian! Oh God, Julian." Kate dropped to her knees beside him. She had such stupid hands; they didn't know what to do. Finally, she plastered one to his forehead and smoothed his hair back. "Tell me what you need. Tell me what to do."

Eyes wild, Julian seemed to look everywhere at once. Tics and jolts pulled at his lips; one eye blinked, then the other. He was a broken china doll, and Kate had always been afraid of china dolls.

"The moon," he whispered.

"What?" Kate tried to follow his line of sight. "What about it? Are you all right?"

The tremors ebbed away, and Julian's gaze turned steady. Knitting his brows, he pointed to the heavens and traced an outline in the air. Then he did it again, his hand pale against the dark of the sky. "There's no moon."

Tipping her head back, Kate frowned at the sky. The stars flickered, silent and watching, always watching. Her head swam, but she tried to stay calm. "I know; it's all right. Can you sit up?"

Julian pushed himself to his elbows and grabbed Kate's lapel to get her attention. Color bled back into his skin, but his voice was still rough, his breaths uneven.

When his brow brushed her temple, a spark passed between them. He curled curious fingers in her hair, tugging the knots loose to free it. The sound he made slipped right into her, one somewhere between fear and confusion.

"It's supposed to be full. And Kate . . ."

"What?"

"All your hair is white."

Fifteen

In the middle of the night, Caleb stood at the window and watched the city go by. The traffic slowed down, but it never stopped. The sidewalks cleared, but they were never empty. Pouring himself another finger of whiskey, he let the glass warm in his hand before he took a sip.

Sleeping on land made him sick to his stomach. Six weeks onshore, he should have been steady by now. But his body still tilted when he walked, trying to make up for waves that weren't there. During the day, he cursed it under his breath and kept moving.

At night, all he could do was keep his own company and keep drinking until he passed out. His skin felt oily slick, and his mouth tasted like burnt popcorn. But unconscious was unconscious, and when he got there by way of bourbon, he didn't dream.

He leaned his brow against the glass. His breath fogged it, and something about that circle of white drew people's attention. A pair of women hustling down the street looked up at the same time. One of them jumped. The other grabbed her friend's arm and dragged her quickly away.

Rolling his eyes at them, he took another sip. Did they think he could grab them from two stories up? Even if he could, he sure as hell didn't care to. Maybe they were a couple of dumb broads, didn't know the difference between a man and a ghost. Vaguely amused, Caleb finished his drink and put the glass aside.

When he looked out again, *he* saw a ghost. Long white hair swirled in the wind, and the face beneath it . . . Cold shock gripped him, and Caleb looked away. He hadn't had that much; he wasn't that far gone.

But he was a sailor, and those that made their living on the sea believed in signs and omens. If he turned around and she was still down there, he wasn't seeing things. She had to be real.

Digging his fingers into his own wrists, he pivoted. And there, beneath a streetlight, she stood. Amelia van den Broek, come back from the dead. She dared to stare at him.

Her gaze bored into him, a diamond-tipped burr that ground through flesh and bone alike.

Pushing her hands into her hair, she sectioned it with brutal efficiency. As she braided it, the silver disappeared into dark. Her lips moved. No matter she was too far away to hear, Caleb heard her. That ghost whispered, and it drifted into his ears. It was a bead of black ink dropped into a bowl of water.

If you tremble, I would fear not. If you tremble, I would fear not. If you tremble, I would fear not.

She taunted him! She taunted him with her old lies, with false prophecies that promised he would have a life and a future distant from all this. A perfect life, with his Sarah at his right hand, perhaps their children at the left. All of it stolen, all of it destroyed by her lies. That ghost glowed beneath the lamplight and *laughed* at him.

Throwing himself at the door, Caleb forgot he wasn't supposed to be in the theatre at night. If the night watchman saw him descend from his secret apartment, he didn't care. His blood boiled, and his teeth were sharp for revenge. Burning and sweating, he crashed into the lobby doors.

Locked, they refused to give way to him, so he pounded the glass instead. It shook as he screamed. He screamed for Sarah, for an escape. He screamed Amelia's name in a curse. And he was screaming still when the police came round.

They stared at him, shaking their heads as the night watch appeared from the side door with his ring of keys.

"All right, pal," one said, closing steel cuffs on Caleb's wrists. "Settle down."

"Been drinking?" the other asked. He sounded friendly enough and didn't twist Caleb's arm as he led him out of the theatre. But he did cuss when Caleb struggled and pulled him to the ground.

"Come back here, Amelia," Caleb roared.

Dragging the cops behind him, he managed a few steps. Muscles stood out, tight and hard in his throat, and he lunged once more toward a ghost that had faded away. "Come back and get what you deserve!"

He was so blind with rage, he didn't see the nightstick coming. And then, all was dark.

Unconscious was unconscious, however he got there.

<hr />

"There was a Help Wanted sign in that window this morning," Julian said.

"Maybe they filled it this afternoon?" Kate said. The moon couldn't be full and new in the same night. The unbearable heat had dissipated in an instant . . . time had passed. A lot of it.

Kate sounded like a liar, and worse, the lying she did was to herself. Julian stole looks at her every so often, concerned. She kept braiding and unbraiding her hair.

He'd been wrong. It hadn't *all* turned white. But instead of one bright tuft, the whole crown was silver. Most of its length was still brown, so when Kate twisted it the right way, the braids alternated colors. White, then dark, white, then dark.

A Packard whipped around the corner, kicking up a mechanical wind. Julian put out a crutch to stay Kate before she walked out in front of it.

Kate smeared a hand across her eyes, then looked up at him. Perhaps it was the white hair, but she seemed *older*. Her features sharper, somehow, the planes of her face more refined. Even her voice sounded richer.

"Okay, explain it again."

Rather than walk on, Julian nudged her closer. "Time outside your . . . your circle, the parts you stopped . . . it must have gone faster the longer we were in there. There was a storm coming, and now the skies are clear. It was due to be a full moon tonight, but look up. There isn't any moon at all."

"That's ridiculous," Kate said. "What would you know about the sky anyway? Do you follow astrology?"

Seeing him die must have addled her brains. It hadn't

done much for him, either. His head split with a headache, and every inch of him burned. But he wasn't wrong; everything had a natural course. He saw it on the farm every day, every month, every year.

Kate had stopped time for two hours, according to his watch. But according to the celestial clock, they'd been gone three weeks.

"There's a difference," Julian said, "Between astrology and astronomy. Look."

Julian rested on his crutches and caught her hand. The constellations weren't so visible in the heart of the city. Too many lights burned through the dark, they swallowed faint stars and fine details alike. He had to guide Kate's hand carefully.

Their arms twined like ribbons around a Maypole. The fit was easy, and Julian curled his fingers into her palm. Raising her index finger to point, he traced her hand across the heavens.

His voice was little more than a murmur when he named the stars for her. "Altair, Deneb, Vega."

"Abracadabra," she replied. "Ish ka bibble. Kalamazoo."

He couldn't help it. He rolled his eyes and released her. Making his way into the street, he informed no one in particular, "If anybody ought to be wound up about this, it should be me."

Kate dashed after him. "How do you figure?"

"My whole life, I thought I was the only one." Swinging onto the curb, Julian moved acrobatically. He raised his feet into his crutches as if they were stilts and turned to face her on them. "Then today, I find you. And you say you know a whole gaggle of witchy people."

"Because I do!"

"Then you should be used to it! I should be the one blibbering my lips and braiding my hair."

Narrowing her eyes, Kate said, "You don't have enough hair to braid."

"I'd grow some, to make my point."

Snapped out of her haze, Kate fell into step beside him. "I bet you would."

They fell silent, trudging along in the dark. Unsettled, Julian kept scouring the street for signs. Maybe he wasn't used to the California sky yet. Maybe storms really did pass that quickly on the ocean. But for all of his maybes, his heart jolted when he saw a newspaper abandoned in the trash.

Hurrying over to it, he picked it up and flipped it over. Even though he'd suspected the truth, it was still a shock. His mouth went dry, and he was suddenly much too hot. Holding it up to Kate, he pointed at the date.

"July fifth," Kate murmured.

With a grim nod, Julian tossed the paper. "It was June seventeenth this morning. Says so on my pay envelope."

"Julian, no. It can't be, it really can't be." Hands flapping like wounded birds, Kate plunged forward. "A month?!"

"More like twenty days," he said, but she ignored him.

"Oh, God, Mollie's going to be steamed."

So far, every conversation he'd had with Kate was like an experiment. It was like she wanted to see how little information she could impart and still be understandable. At the moment, she made no sense whatsoever. Following her slowly, Julian asked, "Who's Mollie?"

"She hates Handsome. Oh no. Oh no, Julian, she hates him so much! How fast can you go? Come on!"

Utterly confounded, Julian sped up a little. Her mental state couldn't possibly shift that fast, but as he disclaimed it to himself, he changed his mind. Of course it could. She kissed total strangers on whim. She wore men's clothes and took pleasure in gruesome things.

He couldn't tell if he liked her or feared her, but he found himself following her all the same.

~~~~~~

Shoving her hair into her hat, Kate slipped into the apartment lobby as quietly as possible. There were rules for tenants of The Ems, a long list of them. And if she remembered correctly from signing the lease, she was breaking most of them.

It was after ten p.m. and she had a guest. Of the opposite sex even, though she was the only one who knew that.

They were halfway up the stairs when the landlord flew at them.

"He must sleep with one eye open," Kate whispered to Julian. Then she tugged her hat down, almost to her eyes. "Sorry, Mr. Riggsby. I know it's past curfew. I missed the last red car, but I promise it won't happen again."

"Your sister said you went back to Montana." Mr. Riggsby's gaze raked over her, then darted to Julian. "Who's this?"

"Our cousin Julian from Montana, of course." Kate put a hand on Julian's arm, her smile sticky-sweet. "It's a surprise. He was always Mollie's favorite, so he came for a birthday visit."

Mr. Riggsby pursed his lips. "Oh really, a birthday visit?"

"Oh yes," Kate said. "She gets very homesick, so Julian — he's so clever — said, 'She doesn't even know I'm back from the war yet. She'll jump right out of her skin.' Isn't that what you said?"

"You have a better memory than I do," Julian said. Then

he winced when she pinched his arm. "Yeah, it was something like that, for sure."

"You wouldn't put an injured veteran out in the cold, would you?"

Quick talking could only get her so far. She could hear her heart pounding in her ears, and every breath she took was a little too loud. For a moment, Kate thought Mr. Riggsby might ask for proof, and what would she do then?

Instead, he crossed his arms. "The rent's due. Your sister's been sneaking out so I can't catch her for it."

Slumping in relief, Kate said, "Tomorrow morning, first thing, Mr. Riggsby."

The landlord shot Julian one more skeptical look before retreating to his apartment. Kate grabbed the railing and bounced up two steps. "That could have been a disaster."

Julian turned to sit, looping both crutches over one arm. "How many flights up?"

"Just one," she said, then watched in surprise as he lifted himself step by step, sliding on his backside the whole way. The crutches tapped against the tile, a long string of Morse code dots.

Uncertain, Kate said, "Do you want me . . ."

"Walk, Kate," he replied. "I would if I could."

So she did, but slowly. It was almost painful, taking measured steps when she wanted to bolt to her door. Standing ahead of Julian, she caught a glimpse of the back of his neck warmed by a blush.

Without thinking, she trailed her fingers over it, and smiled when the skin prickled. It was absolutely mad, but she felt like he belonged to her.

"Do you mind?" he asked.

"I don't." Kate hopped onto the landing and held her hand out to him. "Do you?"

Sliding his crutches past her, he grabbed the rail and her hand, hefting himself to his feet. "Yeah, a little bit, I do."

Kate handed him his crutches, then hurried down the hallway. She wanted to open the door first, peek in and make sure Mollie was decent. Pressing her ear to the door, she listened but heard nothing. No wonder, considering the hour, so she slipped the key in, then caught the door before it swung open.

"Mollie?" she said, softly. All of a sudden, her throat was tight, and she couldn't seem to get a whole breath. For her, the fight on the red car was only hours old. That realization started a waterfall of others.

For Mollie, that argument was almost a month past. From Mollie's perspective, Kate had disappeared after the fight and never come back.

"Mollie," Kate said, and shook the bed. No answer.

Mollie was a light sleeper. That had been her excuse, anyway, when she'd insisted that Kate needed to start sleeping on the floor. So Kate shook the bed harder, an earthquake for a light sleeper. The bed slid, then thumped against the wall. Too easily to have anyone in it: she wasn't there. In the middle of the night, she wasn't there.

Kate flipped on the light.

It blinded at first, but not enough to hide that the bed was empty . . . and so was the room. Dread seeped through her; it was like walking through a spider web. Curtains shivered at the breeze through the open window. It stirred empty envelopes that lay on the dresser, making them crack and whisper.

Brittle, Kate gestured at the window when Julian came in. "She let my bird out."

"I'm sorry." Julian leaned against the door, stepping no farther inside.

Picking up one of the envelopes, Kate felt herself fall as keenly as if she'd jumped from the window. Flapping the envelope at Julian, she said. "The movie I told you about? The film's gone. It's gone."

Kate forced herself to keep looking. There was the tiniest, stupidest hope that somehow Mollie was hiding, that none of this was what it seemed.

No shoes beneath the bed, only her little velvet pillow. As she searched the room, wafts of Mollie's perfume puffed up like ghosts. A great gust of it washed over her when she threw open the armoire.

Clapping a hand over her mouth, Kate fell to her knees.

Not only were Mollie's few things missing, so were Kate's. Her camera. The music box — with all the money.

But the worst was Handsome. He lay on the floor, unmoving. Torn paper surrounded him, droppings too, and orange peels starting to desiccate. His talons clutched nothing but air.

"How could she do something like this?" Kate whispered. Picking him up carefully, she cradled him to her chest. He wasn't as cold as she expected, but he was irrevocably still.

There was nothing pretty or delicate about the way Kate cried. Grief undid her, smearing her mouth and splotching her skin.

Everything was supposed to change when she got to Hollywood, but not like this.

It wasn't supposed to be *hard*; Mollie wasn't supposed to hate her. But now everything was lost. Her equipment, her money — her darling Handsome. Her life had come apart like wet tissue. Clutching Handsome, she sobbed.

Julian hesitated, then to himself muttered, "There's still some red."

It didn't make sense to Kate, and it didn't have to. Julian circled the bed, then slid his crutches beneath it. His hands were gentle, sweeping down her arms. "Bring him here."

Trying to dry her face with her shoulder, she choked down her tears. "No. No, you said it yourself, everything's funny when we're together. What happened on the beach, that wasn't a spell. You were *dead*."

With a brash smile, he tugged on her again. "But I didn't stay that way."

Climbing into bed, Kate was reluctant to give Handsome over. "Is that how you do it? Die a little to bring something little back?"

"I think so." He rubbed his arms briskly, as if he were warming himself to the task. Something flickered across his face, awareness and fear. Swallowing twice, he reached out for Handsome, then said, "Close your eyes, Kate."

"Why?"

"Sometimes they're too far gone. They don't come back right."

Clinging tighter, Kate said, "What about you? Do you come back wrong too?"

When he trailed his fingers down her arm, it felt like a promise. A reassurance. He met her eyes, his own impossibly sincere. "It'll be all right. Trust me on this one."

When Julian's hands brushed hers, she made herself let

go. Tenderly, he settled Handsome in his arms, smoothing the raven's feathers. He took care with him, making it easier for Kate to close her eyes.

In her own darkness, Kate felt Julian draw a deep breath; she heard it slip from his lips. Emotions knotted in her throat, tightened by passing seconds. He'd raised the turtle almost instantly. This was taking so long; it couldn't be good. What did he mean, sometimes they were too far gone? What would happen if Handsome was?

Anxiety stretched the knot from her throat to her belly. She couldn't trade a boy for a bird. It was wrong; she couldn't do it. As she opened her eyes, two things happened. Julian fell back on the bed, motionless. And Handsome flapped his wings and hopped away.

"Nevermore!" he croaked, his black eyes gleaming once again.

Sixteen

Clutching the steering wheel, Amelia veered around a horse cart and honked at a pair of surveyors standing in the middle of the street. A black scarf bound her hat to her head, and her kid gloves were worn to a sheen. Her grip was white knuckled, her jaw set hard.

Thirty days ago, she'd rarely *seen* the inside of an automobile, let alone piloted one. Now she careened through Los Angeles with a cool stare and an absolute disdain for anyone who got in her way.

"The sidewalks are for pedestrians, dear," Nathaniel murmured under his breath.

Amelia cut a look at him. "Don't tell me how to drive. You're the one who ran the Jeffery off the road."

Truth be told, *neither* of them was a good driver. Even

when they had to make do with a victoria, they let the horses wander too far and run too fast. Spoiled by magic, they were people made for slicking across distances by will alone.

Everything else — automobiles, streetcars, trains — moved too slowly.

Hurtling around a corner, Amelia said, "What shall we raise it to?"

"A thousand. Much more than that and we'll end up with pretenders and liars in our suite."

Every week for the past month, they'd run ads in all the newspapers in print in Los Angeles. That hadn't been their first choice; they'd begged for a reporter to take down a story. They'd even offered a miniature to photograph, a cameo portrait of Kate that Nathaniel had painted on her sixteenth birthday.

"I'm sorry, folks," the editor said. "But there's nothing to write about here. The whole city's built on runaways. You can stand down at the train station and watch 'em roll in by the hour."

So they'd advertised instead, at first for any information on the whereabouts of their daughter. Possibly masquerading as a boy, last seen in a plum suit. They got plenty of notes about actual boys — boys working in a hat factory, boys running packages across town. But nothing about Kate at all.

Then they added Julian to the listing. After a flurry of letters and telegrams, Zora and Amelia discovered that their children had run to the same city and that all four parents had lost their gifts at the same time. Perhaps it was coincidence, but it certainly seemed more.

Armed with an address and a directive from Zora to check on Julian, Amelia and Nathaniel presented themselves at Bartow's Ordinary.

"Haven't seen the poor mite in a while," Mrs. Bartow told them. "I thought he might be keeping odd hours, but when he didn't pick up his laundry . . ."

Plenty of people had seen Julian. They followed his trail through the neighborhood but always came back to the Ordinary. Since he'd paid rent for a month, they decided to check back for a month. Either he was truly gone or just . . . away. On a jaunt. Or an adventure.

Or so they hoped.

"I've got a good feeling," Amelia said abruptly.

Nathaniel combed his fingers through his hair. A few threads of silver shot through the dark waves. Enough to make him distinguished, which was far too close to respectable for his taste. Stretching out to pet the back of Amelia's neck, he nodded agreeably, even though he didn't agree.

People who disappeared usually did so for a reason: either they were dead or they didn't wish to be found. There was no pleasure in admitting that, even to himself. No pleasure in hoping that his only child had taken after her parents and fled in the night.

The newspaper building loomed. With car horn blaring, Amelia cut across traffic to claim one of the few open parking spots along the sidewalk. Bouncing off the steering wheel, Amelia jerked the car out of gear and cut the power.

Since that was always how she parked, it never occurred to her that there might be a less emphatic way of doing it. Plucking her handbag off the floor, she shook it at Nathaniel. "I've got a good feeling about today, monster."

Nathaniel caught her chin and tipped her head back for a rough kiss. Her mouth tasted ever the same, and he soothed himself on the part of her lips.

Lingering a moment, he stroked her jaw with his thumb, then murmured, "I hope it comes to something."

~~~~~~~~~

Curled against Julian's body, Kate kept an arm thrown over him. She splayed her fingers over his heart, waiting for its first beat.

He hadn't come back yet, not after a minute, not after an hour. She'd fed and watered Handsome, let him outside to stretch his wings, then returned to her vigil at Julian's side.

Sharing a bed with a boy should have been a monumental occasion, and in a way, it was. The first night she'd slept with the dead. She studied his profile and slipped her hand into his.

As sentinel, it was her sacred duty to keep him safe through the night. Though sleep tried to tempt her, she kept herself awake with pinches and long drinks of water. And then, when he grew cold and stiff, fear made for excellent waking company.

Morning dawned, and he still lay there — too peaceful. His golden hair fell in waves from his brow. His lashes were dark fans on his skin. His lips, drawn with an ornate line, were gray, nearly blue.

He'd told her to trust him, and she did, truly she did. She was starting to think he had trusted himself too much.

"I'm the worst person in the world," she said, pressing her face to his cold shoulder.

In reply, Julian sat up. Heaving, his shoulders flexed and his joints cracked. He sounded like dry kindling. An awful, rattling sound filled the room. He clawed for breath, wheezing and choking. He left dark streaks on his own throat, clutching at it with bloodless fingers.

Terror shot through Kate. She clambered up after him, trying to catch him and hold him. Her thoughts raced — would she know if he was too far gone? How long would he have to lie dead before she could truly judge him finished? And what would she do if he was? What if she made a mistake and accidentally had him buried alive?

As he quaked against her, she held her breath. It kept her from tearing up again, but nothing kept her from hating herself. She loved Handsome with all her heart, but it had been wrong to let Julian die for him.

"It's all right," she said, unconvinced herself. She rubbed him briskly; she kept her brow pressed against his temple. He still felt stiff. It was terrible, like holding a cold, leather doll. "Julian, you're all right. I'm here."

Julian clutched at her, contorting himself to look at her. An eerie film clung to his eyes. He opened his mouth, but instead of words, an awful sound came out. Like the settling of a house or the moan of a tree about to break, it shuddered through him and raised the hair on the back of her neck.

"It's okay," Kate said, but it came out as barely a squeak. Stroking his hair, his face, she willed him better. She demanded it, from the universe, or the sky, or the elements.

Why not the elements? If they were born of aether, and aether was breath, then he should breathe! He should be well!

Clasping a hand to Kate's face, Julian pressed a little too hard, tangled too roughly with her hair. But he blinked, and the haze faded. Not all at once, but gradually. As warmth spread through him, his flesh softened. Blue lips shifted to rose pink again; a dewy blush sprang up in his cheeks.

"Julian, can you say something? Can you hear me?"

For a long moment, he stared. Then, as his fingers slipped from her hair, he croaked, "Course I can hear you. You're right in my face."

Overwhelmed in every sense, Kate snapped. She pushed him back onto the bed, because it wouldn't do to drag him to his one good foot to shake him.

Throwing a leg over, she sat across his hips and truly leaned down in his face. She clasped his head with both hands and peered down at him furiously.

"You can't ever do that again. Promise me."

"Promise you what?" Julian said; his lips still moved a little slowly, but his eyes widened without effort. "Is there a reason you're sitting on me?"

"Because you were dead all night!" Shifting forward, Kate looped her arms around his head, fingers tangling in his hair. He was warm again; his heart pounded on, and she could feel it in her own veins.

"Why don't you ever make sense, Kate?"

Letting out a frustrated yelp, Kate collapsed on top of him. Her hair flowed over his face; his breath slipped hot against her skin. Turning to press against his neck, she sighed. Everything was right again. It had to stay that way.

Reordering her thoughts, she tried to explain herself as clearly as she possibly could, even though he'd probably argue with her anyway. "I was afraid. And now I'm happy. I'm inappropriate, and I don't care. I want you to promise you won't do it again."

Julian raised his hands helplessly, then dropped them on her back. Petting her, he said, "I promise."

"Thank you," Kate said.

"You're not inappropriate, by the way." He blew at her hair, trying to get it off his face. "You're *indecent.*"

"Thank you." Kate nestled down, patting him. "Shhh, I'm trying to sleep now."

Jerking his head up, Julian managed to flounder beneath her weight as he exclaimed, "On me?"

"Shhh," she repeated, and drifted off with a smile.

～～～～

The nap only lasted until Mr. Riggsby came for the rent.

He pounded on the door, jolting both of them into motion. As Kate scrambled to straighten the mess in the armoire, Mr. Riggsby called through the door, "Noon is not first thing in the morning!"

"Who is it?" she called back, stuffing dirtied papers into the trash bin.

"You know who it is!"

Kate tried to hurry. "I know it's a lot to ask, but could I borrow a dollar? Maybe he'll take that as a deposit. The rent's ten a month, and I ought to have a pay packet waiting for me at The Pike."

"Ten dollars?" Julian boggled at her. "For this dump?"

"None of the boarding houses would take us," Kate snapped. "No animals, and no actors! For two people and a bird, it's a steal!"

Eyes trained on the door, Julian considered that for a moment, then shook his head. "Forget it. Come with me. Maybe I can sweet-talk Mrs. Bartow into letting Handsome stay."

Brightening, Kate shoved the rest of the filthy paper into the bin. "Really?"

Mr. Riggsby pounded the door again. "I can hear you! I'm coming in there!"

Julian pulled his crutches from under the bed. Keeping his voice low, he said, "Do you have a fire escape?"

"Yes, but you can't . . ." Kate started, then watched in amazement as Julian pushed the window open and hoisted himself through it. Turning back to look at her, he waved his hand. "Come on."

The door rattled, then a ring of keys jingled. Grabbing her hat and her shoes, Kate flung herself after Julian. They were only one flight up, and Julian had already lowered the ladder.

"How are you going to get down?" she asked.

Thrusting the crutches at her, he said, "Watch this."

Julian pulled his sleeves over his hands, then grabbed the ladder's iron frame. Holding tight, he dropped down, catching one of the rungs with his foot. Once he had his balance, he bounced his way down, the fire escape protesting every jump. Hopping to the ground, he looked up. "Throw me the crutches."

Dropping them, as well as her hat and shoes, Kate scrambled down the ladder. Soft flecks of rust fluttered around them, mixed with fine concrete dust.

"Trying to kill me?" Julian asked. He hooked her hat with the foot of his crutch and tossed it toward her.

Stuffing her hair under the hat, Kate snorted. "Trying to knock some sense into you. Handsome!"

"Yeah, I am," Julian said. Then he turned to look for a familiar black beast on the rooftops or the wires. It occurred to him that he didn't know how he was supposed to tell one crow from another, so he called, "Handsome, come on!"

When the bird swept down to land on Julian's shoulder, Kate blinked. "I can't believe he did that."

Wincing, Julian started down the street. "Me either. Those claws hurt!"

The street sloped downhill, and instead of hopping along, Julian could take long swings between his crutches. Clapping her hat to her head, Kate ran after him.

Mr. Riggsby stuck his head out the window and yelled after them, "Don't come back. You or your sister! Or your cousin. Your entire family is banned!"

"I feel bad," Kate said. "My whole family is banned from The Ems, and it's all my fault."

Julian burst out laughing, then suddenly cursed. A street vendor rolled her cart onto the sidewalk in front of them, its umbrella swinging gaily in the wind.

It happened sometimes, when he got going too fast, that Julian couldn't slow himself down without crashing.

It was fine when he was chasing his brothers around the yard. But colliding with a steaming metal cart, sprawling into traffic — that wouldn't be fine.

Better into a brick wall, he decided, and veered that way. Then something blinked. No, it flickered. Like a hand passing in front of a flame. It took him a moment to realize he wasn't on his feet anymore. He was on the ground, sprawled on the sidewalk with his crutches neatly by his side.

A hand from nowhere grasped the back of his neck, and another flicker passed through his sight. At once, he understood — she'd stopped time again, kept him from falling. Then she'd rearranged him. Instead of hitting the wall he came to, safely on his backside.

Kneeling beside him, Kate dropped her head onto his shoulder and whispered, "Look what I did."

He started to reply, but then he lifted his head. The world hung suspended in a moment. Not a little corner of it, the entire street.

Frozen automobiles stood in half-completed turns. Caught midstep, a couple of businessmen seemed to hover in the air. Steam rose from manhole covers but never dissipated. All the way down the angled street, life had stilled.

"Help me up," Julian murmured.

Climbing to their feet, they moved through the perfect silence. Peeking around the corner, Kate whistled low. She'd caught a boy jumping from the streetcar, a woman snapping a rug from her third-story window.

Julian rubbed his knuckles against Kate's arm. "Wonder how far it goes?"

"I wonder what happens when it all starts again at the edges." She looked up at him. "I never had to turn it off before. I don't know how."

Like a gradual dawning, scarlet spots started to glow for Julian. Some beneath the streets, no doubt vermin. But the city was full of blood-red lights, full of the departed still close enough to call back. He didn't know how there could be so many. His breath faltered to see they were surrounded.

"Do it backwards," he suggested. "Whatever you do to stop the world in the first place.

Kate pulled off her hat and wrung it between her hands. Instead of exhaling a breath, she drew one in, as deep and as long as she could. Her lips moved as she whispered something to herself. Her eyes darted from side to side beneath her eyelids, and then suddenly, she opened them wide.

In the distance, something crashed. A man yelled. Handsome squawked and landed awkwardly on the sidewalk, only to take flight before he got kicked by a passerby. And Julian stared as silver streaked through the rest of Kate's hair. Her black-and-white braids turned entirely white, and her face changed too. It was longer, her lips were fuller, and her jaw sharper.

"What?" Kate said, surprised at the timbre of her own voice. It was still unmistakably hers, just deeper.

Cool realization rushed over Julian as his mother's words in the kitchen came back to him. They were clarion, impeccably clear. They reverberated in his bones, echoed in his blood.

Uneasy, Kate shifted her weight from foot to foot. "Julian, what?"

"You don't stop time," he said. "You trade it."

Raising his crutch, he herded her toward a department store window. With the light cast on it, it made a perfect mirror. When Kate caught a glimpse of herself, she swayed against him.

"I look like my mother."

Julian watched her eyes through the reflection. Smoothing a hand down the back of her neck, he watched as understanding swept through her.

She hadn't lived through stopped time. The people on the streetcar, the woman with the rug, the businessmen who bounded past them now, completely oblivious. They went on with their lives, no older than they were before — because Kate traded against the time she had left in her life to stop *them*.

Pulling Kate in to comfort her, Julian whispered against the shocking white of her hair. "No more, all right? We can — you can get by without it."

"It's not really good for anything anyway," Kate said.

Forcing a smile, she slipped out of Julian's arms and gestured for Handsome. Instead of running, they walked, sometimes more slowly than they had to. When they reached Sixth and Spring Street, Julian pointed at the short house set between two towering apartments.

"Let me talk to Mrs. Bartow first," he said. "You better put your hat back on."

"She wouldn't turn you out with a little brother to take care of," Kate said. But even her fabulating sounded sober for the moment. She held the door open for Julian, then followed him inside.

"Boy, where have you been?" Mrs. Bartow demanded as he approached her desk. "All sorts came looking for you, and I had to send them away!"

A bit baffled, Julian said, "You did? I mean, who was it?"

Opening up drawers, one after the other, Mrs. Bartow produced a thin stack of letters. "A fancy couple, claiming to be friends of your mother's. A little girl, well, not so little — she came twice. I hope you didn't get her into trouble. I'll throw you right out!"

Julian took the letters and swore. "No, ma'am, not ever. I had to fetch my, uh, baby brother."

Slowly, Mrs. Bartow tipped to one side. She blanched when she saw the massive bird that came with the boy. "I might ignore the brother, but not that thing. Birds are filthy, carry lice and whatnot. I run a clean establishment."

In general, Julian wasn't given to fantasy. Kate probably could have come up with a better story, he thought, but they'd have to make do with his. Gesturing at Kate and Handsome, he said, "He's not wild. My brother rescued him from a circus. Fire. From a circus fire. It was terrible. But he's trained — the bird. My brother is too, but that goes without saying."

Suspicious, Mrs. Bartow came around the desk. "What kind of training?"

Julian turned and prayed the bird would go along with the lies. "Handsome, come here."

Hefting her arm, Kate urged Handsome into the air. Filling the foyer, Handsome swooped through the narrow space and dropped himself onto Julian's shoulder. Whether out of habit or because he understood English, he nuzzled Julian's cheek when he settled.

Secretly delighted, Julian reached up to stroke his feathers. "Say something for Mrs. Bartow."

Ever accommodating, Handsome tipped his head to the side and croaked, "I can talk. Can you fly?"

Mrs. Bartow plastered a hand to her own cheek, looking from the bird to Julian then back again. Finally, she shook her head and retreated behind the desk again. "I won't clean up after it. And you tell your brother the rules. One key only. What's his name?"

"Kate," Julian said automatically. Then, before Mrs. Bartow decided to study Kate any closer, Julian blustered, "My parents wanted a girl."

Mrs. Bartow shooed him away. Sitting back behind the

desk, she looked shocked, rather like a train had just missed hitting her.

As Julian led Kate down the hall to his room, he heard Mrs. Bartow repeating in wonder, "I can talk. Can you fly?"

~~~~~~

The desk sergeant dumped a tin tray onto the desk and handed Caleb each item without fanfare.

All around them, the police station buzzed. Beat cops moved through like they were on fire; a whole row of chairs overflowed with people waiting to speak to an officer.

Typewriters snapped along at mad speed, each clack like a nail in Caleb's temple. The welt over his brow had deepened to an impressive shade of purple, and his eye was well and truly black.

He stank of piss and of too many bodies crammed into lockup overnight. He'd spent another night in jail once, for the same damned reason. Amelia van den Broek was determined to ruin his life. All of it, even the miserable end of it.

"One box of matches. Seven inches white twine. Saint Nicholas medal. Tin snips. What in blazes is this thing?"

None too gently, Caleb snatched the silver tube from the sergeant's hand. Its chain whispered when he unfurled it.

Dropping it over his head, he took care to slip the tube into his shirt. It rested cool against his skin, slowly warming by touch. "It's a locket."

Dubious, the sergeant looked him over. But it was obvious he didn't care enough to inquire further. He wouldn't have been interested in the answer anyway — it really was a locket, with one of Sarah's dark curls sealed inside.

"Wallet with two dollars," the sergeant continued, "two dimes, a quarter, and a penny. There you are. Off you go."

Caleb shoved his wallet into his pocket but frowned. "I had some bits of lead."

Flipping open the log book, the sergeant ran his finger down the inventory. Then he laughed. "That's right, three bullets. Sorry, pal, we'll be keeping those."

"The hell you will. That's my personal property."

The sergeant closed the inventory book and leveled a stern look at Caleb. The sergeant wasn't a very tall man, but he was broad. He had shoulders like ham hocks and a jaw so solid, it practically dared someone to take a swing at it. "Look, now. You're free to go. Nobody's pressing charges. Go buy yourself a beer."

"They're fishing weights," Caleb said. Acid swirled in his stomach, burning him from the inside. They both knew he was lying, but he didn't care. Those bullets were his, the same as the change and the twine.

"So you know, there's a ten-dollar fine for fishing without a license, Virgil."

Cussing him to his face, Caleb slapped the desk and backed away. There was no point fighting it. He'd never gotten a fair shake before; he wouldn't get one now, either. Pushing into the afternoon sunlight, he shielded his eyes as they started to water.

Starving, and head splitting, Caleb stopped at the corner. What little he owned was still holed up in the green room at Clune's, and he needed to get it back. He could spend thirty cents on a lunch plate and walk back to the theatre. Or he could take a red car back to Olive Street and beg scraps from Delmonico's kitchen.

A fire engine screamed by. The siren mixed badly with his headache, and Caleb broke out in a cold sweat of nausea. When he recovered, he darted into the road to catch the red car. Sleep first, then scraps.

Then a pint to drown Amelia van den Broek for good.

Seventeen

Curled on Julian's bed, Kate watched him move through his room.

The crutches made a pleasing thump, then his foot whispered across the carpet when he put it down. The slide when he put the crutches away, the sure rip when he split the first envelope in the pile waiting for him. He was musical, entirely unintentionally.

Kate wondered what he'd look like on film. The combination of pale hair and dark eyes would be striking. Would film capture his subtle freckles? Burying her head in her arms, she sighed.

"Letter from my mother," Julian said. Then he laughed quietly, thumbing through the pages. "With an invoice for the money I owe her."

Peeping up, Kate stared. "Your mother bills you?"

"It's a long story," Julian said.

That he didn't want to share, obviously. Kate dropped her head again, closing her eyes. The long night caught up with her, and she wavered halfway between sleep and waking. Trailing her fingers across the quilt, she said, "I need to pick up my pay. Will you go with me?"

"Yep."

"Soon?"

He glanced at her, letters in hand. "Give me a minute."

Kate rolled onto her back and stared at the ceiling. Tender everywhere, she felt like one big bruise. When she'd stepped onto the train to Los Angeles, she'd had doubts, but she also had ambition. And hope. And, she was forced to admit, advantages. Plenty of money, an expensive camera, someone who knew how to find her way around the city.

That was all gone; this was starting over the very hard way. She'd learned to find a job and take the streetcar, so she wasn't helpless. The art in her head still flowed in moving pictures; her yearning to bring them to life hadn't changed. And she had a friend now — a true one.

"What are you sighing about?" Julian asked.

Kate rolled onto her stomach again and propped her head in her arms. "Nothing. What are you frowning about?"

"Nothing," he replied. Tossing a letter onto the table, he leaned back and scrubbed his face with his hands. "Can't believe I lost three weeks"

"I didn't mean for it to happen."

"Didn't say you did."

Kate knotted herself around and came up sitting on the edge of the bed. It didn't seem right that she could have visions of somebody her entire life but have things turn out like this. He should have been madly in love with her; she should have been equally mad for him. What about the stars? A secret wedding, a tangled destiny?

He was pretty to look at, his lips wonderfully warm. But mostly, she wanted to poke him in the ribs and count his teeth and find out if he had webs between his toes. He looked rather sleek, now that she considered it. Soulful eyes, golden everywhere else . . . It was entirely possible he was a selkie.

"Are you sure you can't take your skin off?" Kate asked.

Turning to face her, Julian leaned forward in his chair. "With a sharp knife and some patience, I expect I could."

He was so exasperated, and so serious, and so literal that Kate had to smile. Bouncing slightly on the bed, she got a very dirty look from Handsome. He flew to the windowsill and tapped the glass with his beak. Rolling to her feet, Kate walked over to let him out.

"Letter from a sweetheart?" Kate asked.

Furrowing his brow, Julian put a hand over the mail. "What makes you think that?"

"I can smell the perfume."

With a vaguely sheepish look, Julian quit guarding his mail. Stretching his arms over his head, he popped his shoulders and said, "She's not a sweetheart. She's a girl I worked with at the laundry."

A likely story, Kate thought. "A coworker who sends perfumed letters. That happens to me all the time."

"We had a movie date, but I stood her up."

"Why would you do such a thing?"

"Because I was busy getting mauled at the beach by a crazy girl."

Shoving her hands into her pockets, Kate shook her head at him. What a sad little man he was. "You're not being mauled right now. Go find her."

"It was almost a month ago," Julian pointed out. "I didn't know her very well. She thinks I stood her up and then ignored two notes she left for me."

Kate pushed off the wall. Plucking her hat off the bed, she dropped it on his face. "That's what flowers are for. Chocolates. Firecrackers, if she likes that sort of thing. Apologies — real ones; you do have to mean it — and presents can work wonders."

"Sometimes things happen for a reason," he said, and tossed the hat back to her.

Reclaiming the cap, she put it on and tried for careless. A bit whimsical, not desperate at all. Light, teasing, but not too forward, because she was mixed up inside. "I could be a reason. You should get to know me."

"What does it look like I'm doing?" he asked. Fishing his crutches from beneath the bed, he rose up on them and then pointed her toward the door. "Let's go get your check while the sun's shining."

Maybe she was delirious from lack of sleep, but Kate couldn't stop smiling.

~~~

As many times as he'd been to the State Fair back home, Julian was mesmerized by The Pike. Great wooden roller coasters stretched over the ocean seeming too spindly to be anything but decoration. He watched in wonder as the trains climbed the first hill together, then spun away on separate paths.

Delighted shrieks filled the air, accompanied by a distant calliope and ringing bells. The scent of frying sausages and cotton candy drifted around him, tempting him to taste a bit of everything.

Following Kate through the midway, he watched a berib-boned little girl pluck a plastic duck from a tub. She bounced when she traded it to the barker for a goldfish in a bowl.

"My brother Charlie's a whiz at those," he said as they passed the milk-bottle game. Two boys wound up and pitched. They threw their baseballs as hard as they could and still only managed to knock the top bottle down.

Kate smiled up at Julian. "He must be clever, then. They're all weighted at the bottom."

Julian hadn't realized that, but it made him laugh in ret-rospect. Sam never managed to knock them down, but Charlie did every time. It was one of the skills Charlie lorded over the younger brothers.

A woman in a turban stepped in front of them. She waggled her fingers and spoke in sultry tones. "My mystic eye sees all. Let Lady Freya lift the veil on your future."

"Maybe another time," Kate said, darting around her.

"I'm fine, thanks." Julian couldn't maneuver quite as quickly as Kate through the crowd, but he managed. Pop guns went off in the distance, drowned out by the clatter of the coaster cars racing back to the station.

As they turned the corner, a bell rang. A strongman in a Tarzan suit swung a sledgehammer over his shoulder and pointed to Kate. "Step up, lad. Let's test your muscle. Ring the bell, win a prize!"

"Let me," Julian said. He produced a penny for the barker, holding it out for him. The barker hesitated. "It's awful heavy, son."

"He can handle it," Kate said.

Her eyes sparkled, avidly following Julian's every move. The barker finally took the penny, and Julian let Kate take his crutches. Rubbing his hands dry on his trousers, Julian took the sledgehammer and hefted it.

The sun beat down, impossibly hot, and the salted-sugared wind swirled around him. There was a trick to this one, too — letting the hammer fall before putting any weight behind it.

A grunt escaped him as he heaved the hammer over. Muscles tightened in his back, hands burning against unpainted wood. Moving with the hammer, he forced his strength into it at the last moment. The impact shook through him, and he was rewarded by the clang of the bell.

Hopping back a few steps, Julian threw his hands up with a grin. "And handle it I did."

The barker forgot his façade for a moment and cursed under his breath in surprise. Quickly regaining his composure, he pulled a stuffed rabbit from the display and tossed it to Kate.

"That's mine," Julian told her, biting back a grin. "I'll let you carry it."

"I'll let you wrestle me for it," Kate replied.

After a few more distractions, she stopped in front of the offices. She ran inside, leaving Julian to ponder the relative merits of funnel cakes versus elephant ears. When Kate emerged, he greeted her with one of each.

"You're going to be broke by morning," she said, but she took the funnel cake anyway. They sprawled on a brightly painted bench, tearing bits of fried dough, and blowing their fingers to cool them off.

Relaxing into the warmth and the chaos, Julian tipped his head toward hers. "I have an idea."

"Does it involve a circus fire?"

"Don't get cheeky. It worked, didn't it?"

Refusing to cede the point, Kate waved a bit of cake before popping it in her mouth. "Have you *ever* seen a raven at a circus?"

"No, but I've never seen anybody keep one as a pet either." Dipping a finger into the powdered sugar on Kate's plate, he dotted her nose with it, then sucked his finger clean. "Or a girl in a suit. Or somebody stop time. Seems to me like anything's possible when you're mixed up in it."

"Aww," Kate said.

Julian reached over and flicked the envelope in her front pocket. "How much do you have?"

"Four dollars," she said. "It would have been five, but they docked me for skipping out without notice."

"Will they let you come back?"

Kate tore off another bite, the white spot of sugar still on the tip of her nose. "Afraid not. Guess we're both in the market for a new job."

Finishing the elephant ear, Julian rolled the paper plate into a tube and sat in silence for a moment. Watching Kate when she wasn't looking, he smiled. A silver curl escaped her hat, floating on the breeze like cottonwood seeds.

She was crazy as an outhouse rat and possessed the most disturbed mind he'd ever encountered. But she was bright and full of life. And he was pretty sure the crutches didn't matter to her.

Coming to the city, out of the safety of his home in Indiana, it had been a shock to find out how many people minded. How little they thought he could do. If nothing else, Kate seemed to think he could manage more than he could.

Reaching over, he tugged her ear and said, "Like I was saying, I have an idea."

"What are you waiting for, an engraved invitation? Tell me!"

"Let's pool our money and waste half of it tonight." He

looked around, gesturing with his shoulders. "Ride some rides. Have a couple hot dogs. Try to win a goldfish."

Standing, Kate turned to him and shook her head. "Handsome would eat a goldfish."

"Try *not* to win a goldfish," Julian replied. "You've got something on your nose."

"I know," she said, and bounded away.

She disappeared among the throng, an occasional flash of plum visible between more subtle tweeds. Somehow, even on a packed boardwalk, with balloons and spinners dancing everywhere, she stood out.

A moment later, she swam against the current and threw a hand up to catch his attention. The question was written on her face: *Are you coming?*

"I take it that's a yes?" he shouted, and dove into the crowd after her.

~~~~~~~

They'd been spun and looped, palm-read and age-guessed. They'd ridden the roller coaster over the water and waded by the beach house. And as The Pike started to settle for the night, Kate wasn't ready for it to end. Tugging Julian's jacket, she pointed to the lighted sign ahead.

"Majestic Ballroom," she said. "Let's go for a whirl."

Julian looked down, amused. "Let's not and say we did."

"But I love dancing," she said.

He replied, "Yeah, but I have one left foot."

Glancing down, Kate started to laugh. "The girls could put their arms round your neck and swing a little bit."

"What about a movie instead?"

He pointed at a sign past the ballroom's, flickering in shades of red and white. Music from The Strand competed with the Majestic, two live bands of entirely different varieties, playing along at once. To add to the chaos, people emerged from one to dart into the other, as if they were playing hopscotch.

Puffing up, Kate circled Julian, already heading that way. "I wonder what they're showing?"

"*The Little American*," Julian said drily. No need to wonder when there was a picture card in the display case naming it.

Bouncing, Kate nearly careened into him. "Oh, Mary Pickford! She was amazing in *A Romance of the Redwoods*. Did you see it?"

"I've never seen a movie at all."

Kate might have been less surprised if Julian claimed to have never seen the sun. Thrilled with the prospect of showing him the electric perfection of a motion picture, she reached back and tugged his sleeve.

"I can tell you absolutely everything about them. What do you want to know?"

With a gentle smile, Julian shook his head. "I wouldn't know where to start."

"You have to start with D. W. Griffith," she said, very seriously. "He makes epics. Like *Intolerance* — oh, Julian. Thousands of extras — those are people who stand around, filling out a scene. Each story had its own tint! And Julian, he constructed ancient Babylon! The whole thing!"

"Sounds grand."

Digging in her pocket for quarters, Kate shook her head. "It bankrupted him. But who cares about money? It was art. Extraordinary art; when you watched it, you traveled through time. It's exactly what I want to do."

Julian produced a handful of change of his own and gave it to Kate to sort. "Go bankrupt?"

"Make art. Paint in light and motion." Kate pulled out all the quarters and handed the rest back to him. "I have ever so many ideas. I want to write a new story for Ophelia. I want to make a film about Joan of Arc, and Persephone, and Mary Magdalene . . ."

Julian stepped into line with her. "Why not blessed Mother Mary?"

"Because she was perfect. Where's the fun in that?"

The theatre's doors swung open. The people who poured out were animated, so bright as they talked about the movie and decided their next destination.

Suddenly, strawberry curls caught Kate's eye. Growing very small in her own skin, Kate paled when Mollie emerged on the arm of a sailor.

Wrapped in watery blue silk and wearing a brand new hat, Mollie threw her head back to laugh at something the sailor said. Even amid the rush, Kate made out the scent of her perfume.

Wrenched from the inside, Kate moved before she could think too much. She caught Mollie's elbow and said, "Where's my camera?"

Awareness flared in Mollie's eyes, then disappeared like a dying ember. "I'm sorry, do I know you?"

The sailor tried to step between them. "Move along, pal."

"Tell me where the film is," Kate said, craning around the sailor. She didn't care if Mollie's date took a swing. Let him do it, let him draw a crowd and make a scene. The police would sort it out; they could get her camera back, her film, her *chance*.

Mollie steeled herself, no hint of warmth in her expression at all. "Leave him alone, Alfred. He must have seen my little picture at the nickelodeon. Fans are so tiresome."

"You *sold* it?" Kate murmured. She felt Julian's hands on her now, strong on her shoulders. Everything felt distant and unreal. "You sold my movie?"

Pulling the sailor back against her side, Mollie gathered herself. "The poor thing's out of his mind. I'd sign an autograph for you, but I haven't got a pencil. Best of luck, though."

Then she glided away with Alfred, too cool to look back. Staring after her, Kate slumped against Julian, hot tears in her eyes. Her first feature, playing in a nickel slot machine without her name on it. It wasn't fair that she could care about Mollie so deeply and Mollie couldn't care less.

Kate wanted to fall to the ground and tear her clothes and cry. She wanted the skies to open up and, for a moment, the whole world to weep with her. But wishing for things like that was useless. It was fantasy, and wasted emotion.

Trying to collect herself, Kate swiped her dry cheeks to make sure no tears encroached. It didn't matter. She had already decided to start over. From the bottom, the very hard way. With a real friend nearby this time, someone she could trust.

"Was that your muse?" Julian murmured, surreptitiously rubbing his knuckles down Kate's spine.

Swiping again, Kate shook her head. Scraping the last of her sentiment away, she turned to Julian and abandoned that past by choice.

"No," Kate said, summoning a rueful smile. "That was an actor."

Eighteen

In the darkness of the red car, Julian slipped his hand into Kate's. His touch didn't interrupt her discourse on making motion pictures, but it did soften her manic gleam.

Whatever a muse was, and he couldn't say he knew how one would fit into modern life, he knew Kate was hurting. That, he recognized from experience; all he could do was squeeze her hand and wait for it to pass.

"That's a ways off now," Kate said finally. She took off her cap and let her braids fall to her shoulders. "Have to get a new camera, don't I? Where did you plan to look for work?"

Julian shrugged, trailing his thumb against hers. "Not sure. A lot of places won't have me. There's got to be something, though."

Leaning her head back against the seat, Kate pondered the ceiling. "Can you drive?"

"A horse cart? Yep. But I can't load one."

A thoughtful sound escaped Kate's lips. She rocked with the red car's motion, her long lashes fluttering as she thought. "Can you sew?"

"Pretty well."

"That's something to start with." Kate nodded, as if she knew the first thing about finding work with a needle and thread. "Are you artistic at all?"

"I play the fiddle." Julian sprawled next to her. There was nothing of note on the ceiling. Dirty fingerprints, a bit of cracked paint. But it was pleasantly dark after the lights from the boardwalk. "Don't have one with me, though."

Kate said, "You can save up for one. I'm saving for a camera now; we can both have a goal."

"Good idea," he said. Her hand was smooth in his, impossibly soft. The scent of smoke and fried food clung to her clothes, but he enjoyed sitting with her all the same. The one thing he truly missed from home was living with his family.

The white farmhouse was only quiet at night, and sometimes, not even then. Kate did an admirable job of making up for the amount of conversation he would have enjoyed with three brothers and two parents.

His visions of her seemed laughable now. The girl in the

dark shared Kate's face, but she'd always been an idealized creature. Someone mystical waiting for him in a surreal place. He never would have guessed the truth. She was a faint reflection of a real girl, and the real girl was far more interesting.

The bell rang, and the red car shuddered to a stop. Julian gave Kate's hand another squeeze, then untangled himself. She leapt from the car, the thick, silver coils of her braids bouncing with each step. She reached for Julian's crutches.

Tossing them to her, Julian swung off the car by the rail. They moved fluidly together, waiting for a break in traffic to hurry across the street. Keeping pace with Julian, Kate whistled a few notes and looked over at him. "Can you play *anything* on a fiddle?"

"If I have the sheet music," he said. "And I know a lot of songs by heart."

Kate chewed her lower lip. "I wonder what would happen if I made a motion picture that matched up with a song. Could you write something new?"

"Probably. What're you cooking up, Kate?"

Doffing her hat, she bowed to him from the corner, then turned on her toes. "A Katherine Witherspoon film, with original score by Julian Birch."

Julian laughed, herding her along with his crutch. It was late; he was tired. The night had cooled, tracing a shiver across his skin. Nothing seemed more appealing at that moment than crashing into bed and drifting away beneath the sheets. "I don't want to be famous."

"Then what do you want?" she asked, pulling open the boarding house door for him.

A wave of homey scents greeted them: pot roast and potatoes, floor polish and pipe smoke. Breaking the quiet, Mrs. Bartow's voice rang out.

"There he is," she said.

Julian hesitated as a man and a woman turned in unison to face him. For the briefest moment, his lips went numb. He didn't recognize the man, but the woman was unmistakable. The dark eyes, the curve of her mouth . . .

Before Julian could say anything, Kate pushed around him and gaped.

"Oh my God, those are my parents!"

~~~~~

Caleb had nowhere to go. Clune's had let him come in long enough to collect his belongings. He didn't have much — a change of clothes, two bullets, and a deck of cards. But by God, they were his.

He tied it all in a bundle, and glowered as the manager

put him out the back door, like a dog. They weren't interested in explanations or apologies or any damned thing at all.

Still rank from the lockup, he'd tried to wash in the public fountain. All he managed to do was soak his shirt before he had to run.

The cop who patrolled Central Park spotted him first thing and swung his nightstick lazily to make a point as he approached.

Slinking away, Caleb had to haul his dungarees up every few steps; everything he owned weighed down the pockets.

So he lightened them a bit, spending the last of his money on whiskey. It fortified him in deep swallows, warming his belly even as it growled for food.

The restaurants weren't in much of a giving mood. After trying all the regular back doors and soft-touch cooks, he still ached with hunger.

With no one looking, he dug into the trash behind one steakhouse and produced a couple of half-eaten baked potatoes. Better than nothing; he gulped them down and scrubbed his hands dry on his pants.

Sick of moving, he wandered Sixth Street. There were plenty of apartments and boarding houses there, so he snuck in to sleep in their lobbies.

A few times, he caught a nap before they shooed him away. The Hotel Alexandria was so damned snooty, he didn't get past the front doors.

Silas had mentioned a halfway house where he could get a hot meal and a dry bed, if he was willing to listen to a sermon. His head still ached from the night before; trying to summon the details from his memory actually hurt.

Clinging to a lamppost, Caleb stared into the dark with bleary eyes. The weal on his brow throbbed, sending sharp waves right into his head. Blinking slowly, he wondered what would happen if he passed out on the street.

Most of the bastards in this city would step right over him, he figured. If somebody called the police, he might end up in the drunk tank. Or better, the hospital. They'd give him a bed in the hospital. A hot meal, maybe a bath.

He cursed under his breath when a red car clattered to a stop up the street. He hated those things; he hated the city. All its sound and all its bodies, the filthy street that never swayed under his feet. The air full of people's cooking and people's stink, and sidewalks full of the same.

When the car passed, Caleb stilled. The ghost was back.

She floated down the street, silver snakes writhing around her head.

Swirling and turning in the night wind, her lips moved, and he swore he could hear her say, *If you tremble, I would fear not.* Drifting into one of the buildings, she left behind only an impression, a glimpse of the past.

A flash of heat burned through Caleb. It burned clarity into his dizzy head and calm through his uncertain belly.

Shoving off the lamppost, Caleb walked into traffic as if he were invulnerable. In the wake of screeching tires and honking horns, he reached the curb and kept going.

With a sure and certain purpose, he pushed open the door at Bartow's Ordinary and stepped into the past. She was there, the ghost all silver; but the living Amelia van den Broek was as well. She hadn't changed, not in twenty years, and Caleb trembled when he realized who stood at her side.

Witherspoon.

That bastard escaped the fire after all. Everyone had escaped that summer except for him. Except for Sarah.

Caleb could hear her laugh still, and the sound of a bowstring singing. This was meant to be. This moment was written in the stars, because how could he catch a mystic by surprise? He had gone free for this, sailed the seas restlessly until now for this.

It was destiny. It was time.

Pulling his gun from his pocket, Caleb drew back the hammer.

Julian moved first. All he saw was a man with a gun.

Chucking the foot of his crutch into his hand, he swung it. The deafening report of a pistol cracked through the lobby. Burnt black powder singed the air.

Jolted by the impact, Julian dropped his crutch when the man hit the floor.

Ears ringing, he staggered toward the man's motionless body and knocked the gun away. It spun across the tile with a hiss.

Everything came too fast for Julian to be afraid; his head was too full of echoes to hear. Nothing kept him from looking; the details came in brighter shades than his usual sight.

Blood slipped from the man's nose, dripping into the dark mat of his hair. Mottled bruises stretched across his face like a mask; his jaw seemed out of place. Through cracked lips, his teeth seemed impossibly jagged, their edges marked with more blood. He was still, but Julian knew death intimately enough. The man's belly rose and fell, faintly, but steady. He was still alive.

Breaking away from her parents, Kate threw herself at Julian. She searched him with desperate hands, tugging his jacket open.

"Are you hurt? Are you crazy? What were you thinking?"

Someone was screaming, and Julian didn't know who. Running past him, into the street, Mrs. Bartow cried for the police. The roaring in his head burst, a void that filled with sound, too much of it. Roused by the shot, the rest of the boarding house pressed into the halls and onto the stairs. They murmured, clutching their robes and slipping closer.

"Julian," Kate's mother said, rising to her feet, "get your things. You're coming with us."

Gasps raced around the lobby as one of the doors swung open. Mr. Kiedrowicz staggered into the hall. At first, it seemed like he carried a bundle of towels. But as he came closer, a little foot flopped out. It was ashen, a stark contrast to the blood blooming through the linens. Screams flooded the hallway, a grieving wail that went on and on.

Unsteady on his feet, Julian couldn't help but figure the sums. He'd struck the man with the gun; he'd turned that shot. It was meant for one of them — instead, he'd sent it off course. The black halo around the hole in the wall stared at him, unblinking. Accusing.

Julian could live with a lot of things, but he believed in consequences. His mother had warned him that he couldn't disturb the course of the world. Now he had, and at a terrible cost.

But he could right it. What he had taken, he could return.

Tucking his crutch beneath his arm again, he moved to meet the grieving man.

"I can fix it," Julian said.

Mr. Kiedrowicz stared at him. His mouth hung open, his eyes tormented. He clutched the bundle in his arms as if he might fall down and die.

"We promised," Kate said, digging her fingers into Julian's arm.

He knew just what she meant: no more powers. No more time, no more resurrection. Just them and their ordinary lives, going along as most people did. Looking down at her, he almost spoke, but he didn't have to.

All he needed to know, he read in her eyes. She nodded, steadying him as he held his hands out for the baby. Smoothing a hand up the back of Julian's neck, she whispered, "I'll stay with you. I can give you a few more minutes."

With a nod, Julian turned back. "You can trust me, Mr. Kiedrowicz. Let me make this right."

The child's crimson glow was still bright but fading fast. Julian looked to Kate's parents. Kate looked just like her mother, all but for the eyes. Those were her father's, through and through. An ache welled in Julian, and he chose his words carefully, every one precious.

"Do me a favor. Please write to Zora and Emerson Birch, Connersville, Indiana. Give them my love, would you?"

"I will not," Kate's mother said. "You'll tell them yourself. Kate, get over here right now."

"Take care of Handsome, okay? I'll see you soon." Kate pressed her fingers to her lips and blew her parents a kiss. Then, before they could stop her, she spilled out her breath. Time collapsed in a tight sphere, swallowing her, Julian, and the baby. She'd made a space just big enough to contain them and nothing else.

All at once, the lobby was empty. Silent.

Handing Kate the baby, Julian dropped his crutches. "We better sit down. Once he's back, you slide him through fast. I only need a minute."

"We're taking as long as you need," Kate said. She sank down beside him, watching Julian's face as he settled in. Her hands shook a little, but her face was serene.

Julian wondered if she didn't realize yet. He wouldn't wake up this time. This was an even trade, his life for Mr. Kiedrowicz's baby — a life lived, if only for seventeen years, in exchange for one barely started.

Still numb, Julian worked his magic by rote. A deep breath in, and he blew it out slowly. As the life drained from him, sensation rushed in to fill the emptiness. There was a flare of joy when the baby started to cry; it was such a clear and perfect sound.

Then despair when Kate took the baby, careful to wrap

him in his blankets, then pushed him from their circle. No doubt in the lobby, people cried out again. Kate and Julian had disappeared in front of them, and now Mr. Kiedrowicz's wounded child reappeared alone, whole and well.

Raising his head, Julian's dark eyes met Kate's. Every raw part of him was exposed at once, and his heart pounded furiously. Mockingly, because as soon as she set time free again, it would stop. His lips felt so dry, like they might crack and only dust would slip from them. But instead, his voice did.

"I'm afraid, Kate."

Kate threw her arms around him, and she pressed her face against his hair. Her warmth spread like a promise. She rocked him gently, murmuring, "You don't have to be. We can stay as long as you want."

"You have to get back," Julian said. He hated himself, because he didn't want to say it. He didn't want to be noble or good. He didn't want to find out what happened when the nothing came and never left.

Whispering behind his ear, she said, "We promised we wouldn't use our gifts again. Well, you did, and now I'm going to. We're breaking that promise together."

Julian squeezed his eyes closed. "Kate, I'm not coming back this time."

"Neither am I."

And there it was; she'd said it and made it real. They could pass three months together in a single night when her magic surrounded them. She intended to let a lifetime pass this time. To stay with him, sharing the end with him, instead of sending him to meet death alone.

When time stopped, silence was perfect. If no one spoke, if no one breathed, it was very nearly nothing — except there was light. Bathed in light, Julian leaned back against her. "You should go. You've got a picture to make. Handsome will miss you."

Kate pulled his hair. "Don't remind me."

It was so very her, what little he knew of her. Choking on a laugh, Julian asked, "Why aren't you afraid? Have you been afraid even once in your life?"

"Yes, but I'm not now."

"Don't tell me you think we're going to heaven."

"I've never been to Sunday school, so that would be a lie." She tugged his ear, then brushed her nose against it. She felt like silk; the brush of her skin, the kiss of her touch. "But I know we're going somewhere."

Julian frowned. "How can you know that?"

"You told me."

He couldn't believe he was going to argue with her, not

now. But that's what he did, turning to look at her incredulously. "When did I ever?"

Assured, Kate started to let her braids out. Every strand was silver now; it swirled like moonlight, cascading around her face and making her ethereal. "'Sometimes they're too far gone, and they come back wrong. They don't stay.' You said that."

"That's not . . ."

"If they have to be close, that means they have to be close to us. Here, with the living." Freeing another braid, Kate fixed him with a look. "If they're too far gone to bring them back, then they must be somewhere else."

"But I don't know where that is, what that is. That's not even good logic, Kate."

"It's not logic. It's faith."

"You just said you've never been to Sunday school." Julian shivered, something stirring beneath his skin. It was sparks or stars, or maybe the end creeping through him in spite of Kate's magic.

Sitting the rest of the way down, she crossed her legs and pulled him to rest his head in her lap. Trailing her fingers over her face, she looked into his eyes.

"So? I still have faith. In you. In the elements. In the universe. What are the stars made out of? How did they get there?"

Julian reached up, twining a lock of her hair around his finger. "I don't know."

"I think we're about to find out," she said. Then she leaned down and kissed him, sharing her heat with him; trading a breath with him.

"What was that for?" he asked when Kate drew back.

With a brash smile, she shrugged and said, "In case I'm wrong. Are you ready?"

"I don't know."

Brushing his hair back, she murmured, "I can feel it moving now. Time getting away from us."

A rush of panic filled Julian. "You should go — let go, Kate."

"Are you ready?"

He shook his head. Time didn't move in his veins like it did in hers. For him, this was one short moment, and all he had. He didn't sense the days that passed in a kaleidoscope flicker. His bones didn't realize that the world they knew was already gone.

In this shimmering shell of magic, they had already outlasted decades.

Calm, Kate brushed his hair back again. Her fingers rested on his skin, warm and certain. With a faint smile, she said, "Tell me you're ready, and I'll let go."

Clasping the back of her neck, Julian closed his eyes and

breathed one more time. He touched her skin and listened to her breath. He pressed his other hand to his own chest to feel his heartbeat. That was all that was left of this life, those little evidences.

After a long moment, he opened his eyes and said, "Count of three?"

"Three," she said.

Sunrises and sunsets glimmered through the lobby windows like so many fireflies. Seasons and years and centuries slipped away, a long dusk that turned to night.

"Two," he replied.

"One," they said together, and there were the stars. The elements. The universe.

THE END

Acknowledgments

Many thanks to my editor, Julie Tibbott, without whom *The Vespertine* would still be a trunk novel and *The Elementals* would never have existed at all. You're Kate and Julian's midwife and godmother — quite a balancing act!

Huge thanks to Jen LaBracio, Jenny Groves, and the entire team at Harcourt. You're incredible, and I'm so lucky that my books are in your capable hands. Thank you so, so much for championing them!

All my love and affection to my agent, Jim McCarthy, who knows all the things, settles all the distress, and answers all the questions. Thank you for being there always.

I owe so much to Aprilynne Pike, Carrie Ryan, Sarah Rees Brennan, Sarah Cross, Sarah MacLean, Christine Johnson, Kay Cassidy, Megan Crewe, and Jackson Pearce that they may as well own me. Call in your markers any-time, ladies.

More effusive thanks go to Jenny Martin, for helping me unearth 1917 Los Angeles, Stephanie Burgis and Samantha Cheh for suggesting *La Belle Dame sans Merci,* and Jeri Smith-Ready for sorting the sky.

Many thanks to Judy Blume for every book she has ever written and for every story that I now remember as my own. Uncle Feather has a soul mate in Handsome.

Sneaky thanks to Katie B., Sophie R., and Heidi Z. If you've gotten this far, you should see how much your friend-ship and support mean to me. If not, I promise you, it's im-measurable.

Special thanks to my mother, Sheryl Jern, whose own battle with polio informed and shaped Julian's story — just as she informed and shaped me as a human being. I hope I've done you justice on both counts.

And always, eternal thanks to Jason and Wendi. I couldn't do this without you, and I wouldn't want to try. Thank you for framing my world.

Finally, thank *you,* my friend. Can you believe we've fin-ished a trilogy together? Thank you for being there all along, for reading, for all your kindness. Thank you for making these characters real.